Last Chance Reunion

Last Chance Ranch Book 4

Liz Isaacson

feel good fiction

LIANA ROBINSON

ISBN-13: 978-1638761488

Chapter One

S issy Longston adjusted the temperature in the brand new administration building, the air conditioner actually working a little too well. She hadn't dressed for such chilly conditions, and she wished she had a sweater to put on.

To remedy her icy hands, she stepped outside into the brilliant California sunshine. May really was the most beautiful month in the state, and she faced east, out into the openness of Last Chance Ranch.

She took a deep breath, the good, earthy smell of the air clearing her mind. Well, at least a little. She worked long hours, yes, but she sure did love the ranch she'd landed at a couple of years ago.

She'd usually had a seething, insatiable need to move on after two or three years, but she didn't see that happening here. Maybe her gypsy heart and wandering spirit had finally found a place to call home.

She inhaled and exhaled again, her fingers and toes tingling as they warmed up beneath the sunshine. She pulled out her phone and logged into the dating app she'd started using a few months ago. She wasn't terribly active, and most of the time, men messaged her and she didn't get it for days.

But she'd been chatting with someone named CowboyDan, and he'd asked her out three days ago. *Just dinner*, he'd said. *Nothing fancy. If it's a no, it's a no.*

She'd liked that he wasn't too terribly clingy, but she still hadn't answered him. The reason was Tom Rosser, the man she'd been out with a couple of times now. She hadn't spent a whole lot of her adult life dating, choosing instead to buy airplane tickets and travel the world, but she knew she couldn't go out with more than one man at a time.

Tom was good-looking and sweet, but the spark between them felt like one of those cheap fireworks children lit. Fire and pop for about fifteen seconds. Then just smoke, darkness, and a bad smell.

She tapped out a quick message to Tom, hoping to let him down easy. *I'm sorry. I don't think this is working out. Thanks for everything.*

Tom had bought her two meals and driven up to the ranch once to pick her up when her car wouldn't start.

She'd had Hudson look at it since then, and it was humming along just fine now.

Sissy sighed, her head pounding, and she hoped she wasn't coming down with a summer cold. After all, there was nothing worse than being sick when the weather was good.

"Hey, Sissy," Amber called, and Sissy lifted her hand in a wave. Amber was a pretty woman who had taken to wearing a cowgirl hat whenever she wasn't in the volunteer building. Sissy had been going to goat yoga every morning for months, simply to be around people. She'd never had any problem fitting in, but she was starting to wonder if she'd been focusing on all the wrong things, for far too long.

She'd always put adventures and experiences above relationships. Having a home, a family, or a husband had never been a priority—until now. And at forty-three-years-old, she feared she'd waited too long. Visited Greece one too many times when she should've gone out with Tanner Duplaix instead.

Or Dave Merrill. The thought poisoned her mind, and she tried to push it away. She and Dave had started at Last Chance Ranch in the same week, and she'd almost quit. But she'd liked Scarlett too much, and she had nowhere else to go. Her two weeks notice had already been put in at the corporation where she led the accounting department.

She didn't want a life in the city. So she'd stayed. Dave simply avoided her, and she didn't speak to him. Or look at him at ranch functions. If she saw him coming, she made a detour. It was a system that had worked for almost two years.

She knew she'd hurt him all those years ago. They'd been serious—diamond-ring serious—and she'd even worn his ring for a week before giving it back and breaking up with him.

She lost track of him after that, but the man wasn't stupid. He knew she'd gone back to her old boyfriend—not that that relationship had panned out. Sissy had disappeared to South America for a month after everything, and she'd come back to a different job. A new adventure.

Now, she was just tired.

She navigated to CowboyDan's message and said, *I'm free tonight. Doable?*

He didn't respond right away, and she went back inside to work through the budget for Horse Heaven. They'd gotten seven new equines from Forever Friends, and that meant several more mouths to feed.

Scarlett Adams, the owner of the ranch, trusted Sissy to approve budgets and make sure the ranch had enough money coming in to maintain animal care and staff salaries. She and her husband, Hudson, had worked tirelessly to make Last Chance Ranch into what it was, and the ranch, the animals, and the people who lived here were thriving.

Sissy didn't live on-site, but about three out of every five days, she wished she did. It warmed her heart to see so many people building lives here, and she'd witnessed three weddings last year. Scarlett and Hudson lived in the homestead, and everyone loved them.

Adele and Carson were the ranch's cutest couple, and they lived in a tiny cabin next to Gramps on the edge of the homestead's lawn, and Sissy may or may not have had to fight off the jealousy every day as she drove by the house Jeri had built for her and her husband, Sawyer to live in.

The two-story beauty sat just a few feet inside the fences of the ranch, right on the main road, and Sissy had never wanted a house as much as she wanted that one. It was then that she'd realized she *did* want to be a wife, a mother, and a homeowner, all things she'd never done in her life.

Not even once.

The door to the administration building opened, and Sissy looked up from her desk though there was a lobby and she was working in her office. No one else worked here, though, so if someone had come, they'd come to see her.

She arrived in the lobby just as Dave said, "This is the admin building. Our accountant works here." He turned to leave, his eyes catching on hers.

They both froze. His voice had done that to her, and she watched the storm roll across the man's handsome features. It seemed impossible that she'd had a hold over his heart for all these years, but he scowled at her and added, "Here she is. Cecilia Longston."

The other cowboy with him stepped around Dave, and Sissy almost went into cardiac arrest. "Gray?" she asked.

"Oh, you two know each other?" Dave looked back and forth between Sissy and Gray as a smile spread across Gray's face.

"We sure do know each other," Gray said, swaggering forward and tucking his shirt into his jeans, though it was already tucked perfectly fine. "We went out two or three times a few years ago." Gray leaned against the desk in the lobby. "How are you, Sissy?"

"It was twice," Sissy clarified for Dave as well as Gray. "Five years ago. And I'm fine."

Dave's jaw clenched, and she wanted to make him relax. She'd do anything to get him to forgive her. Her heart wailed it was beating so fast under the weight of his glare.

"Gray's our new hire," Dave said, his voice definitely on the stiff side.

"And what will you be doing here at Last Chance Ranch?" Sissy asked.

"Agriculture specialist," he said as if he'd just been elected President of the United States.

"You have a degree in that, I believe," Sissy said, hearing the quick intake of air from Dave's direction. She looked at him, silently begging God and him to hear her prayer.

Please forgive me.

Help him to forgive me.

"That's right." Gray's gaze dripped down Sissy, and she didn't like it. Not one little bit.

"Well, we have to go," Dave said. "Loads more to see, man." He tapped Gray on the shoulder, glared one last dagger at Sissy, and turned to leave the building.

Gray lingered, and even went so far as to ask, "Are you single, Sissy? Want to go to dinner tonight?"

Dave spun back toward them, his whole face dark and dangerous. How he could make her heart pitter-patter still, all these years later, wasn't lost on her. They'd met when he was still active in the Army, and she'd fallen fast for him. Fast, and hard.

But she'd always had so many doubts, especially when she was younger, and she'd barely been twenty-five when Dave had proposed. She'd seen nothing of the world. Experienced nothing but college and a boring job in a boring No-Name Hollywood office.

Going back to Teddy had been a mistake. But Dave hadn't heard any of those explanations. Once she'd broken off their engagement, he'd cut off all contact.

"I'm busy tonight," she said with a smile, silently begging Gray to *just go. Please go.* "Sorry, Gray."

He knocked twice on the desk in front of him and opened his mouth to say something else.

Dave got to him first, saying, "Dude, come on. She's busy, and we've got other places to be."

Their eyes met again, and Sissy mouthed the words

Thank you to him. Dave didn't react at all, other than to turn and walk out of the building, Gray behind him this time.

Sissy sagged into the doorframe, the adrenaline coursing through her the only thing keeping her upright.

But hey, progress—Dave had done something for her. Said her name without biting it off and spitting it out.

Her phone bleeped out the three-toned alert that she'd gotten a message on Christian Catch.

Sure, CowboyDan said. *I'm free tonight.*

Sissy smiled at the message, turning to go back into her office, glad the air conditioner had stopped blowing. She spent the next twenty minutes making arrangements to meet CowboyDan in a red sweater at a popular bistro in Pasadena, close to where she lived.

She never met men anywhere but Scooter's, as she knew a couple of waitresses there, and they were always busy.

With a date with a new man—someone she'd had good online conversations with—on the horizon, she managed to put both Dave and Gray out of her mind.

For a few minutes, at least.

Then Dave came roaring back, just like he had been for eighteen years now.

Chapter Two

David Merrill had drawn the way short stick when he'd been assigned to take Gray Lennox around the ranch. He hated the tours in general, but this guy was a real piece of work. He'd flirted with every woman he'd come in contact with, making Dave—who'd been out with fifteen women in the past two years—seem like he never got off the ranch.

As he sweated beneath his cowboy hat, Gray sauntered along next to him. "Does she have a boyfriend?"

Dave employed all of his patience. "Not that I'm aware of."

"She and I, we did go out," Gray said, as if Dave had challenged him on the point.

"Congratulations," Dave said, unwilling to get into a game of who was better between the two of them. Dave had dated Sissy for eight months before asking her to marry him. She'd cried and kissed him, and he could still feel the way she fit perfectly in his arms.

The anger he carried wasn't healthy, and he knew it. It had been a very long time, and while he'd gotten over Sissy, moved on, dated other people, he'd never gotten married. Never asked another woman to marry him.

And he'd lost serious girlfriends because of it. Two of them had actually accused him of having commitment issues, which he supposed he did.

On their way to Horse Heaven, he pulled out his phone and messaged BrainyGirl, the woman he'd been messaging through the Christian dating app he'd found about a month ago. Not that Dave had trouble getting a date. He'd been out with over a dozen women, most of them from right here at Last Chance Ranch.

He wasn't looking for serious. He had band practice a couple of times a week, and he wanted to be social in the evenings. It wasn't a crime to ask a woman to dinner or a movie, have someone to spend his down time with.

He didn't hold hands with everyone, and he hadn't kissed any of the last several women he'd been out with.

When he'd first come to Last Chance Ranch, he'd told Sawyer he didn't want to be set up, and he was fine on his own. Both were true. He had no problem getting his own dates, and he simply didn't want to get married.

Even if the bride were Sissy?

But the bride will never be Sissy, he argued with himself. *So it's a moot point.*

"Do you think I could ask her out again?" Gray asked.

"Sissy?" Dave scoffed, his thumbs flying over the screen to make plans with BrainyGirl. "I don't know why you'd want to, but sure. Ask her out."

"You don't like her?"

"It's...she's fine," he said, unwilling to say anything too negative about her. "She's not my type, but hey, if you like her, by all means, ask her out." Just the thought of Sissy going out with Gray made his blood boil, and he had no right to feel that way.

She'd made it quite clear how she felt about him, breaking their relationship right in half, even though she'd cried. Then she'd left town, and Dave had to find out through a mutual friend that she'd gone right back to the boyfriend she'd had before they'd started dating.

That had hurt the most. He'd wanted to march right to her house, pound on the door, and demand to know what she was thinking. But he'd been stationed in Virginia at the time, and that was a long way from California.

He finished making his date with the woman he'd been getting to know online, hoping she'd be as charming in real life as she was on the screen.

"There you are," Hudson said, and Dave shoved his phone in his back pocket. "You must be Gray."

"Hudson Flannigan," Dave said. "He's the foreman over Horse Heaven."

"Dave's over the llamas," Hudson said. "He tell you that?"

"We haven't made it to LlamaLand yet," Dave said.

"And he's a bit sore he didn't get the dogs." Hudson grinned at Dave like it was so funny he'd wanted Canine Club and had lost the game of rock, paper, scissors to Cache. The man already had his hands full with the cattle, and Dave got assigned as second-in-command over the canines. So it was still acceptable to him.

Lance Longcomb was foreman over Piggy Paradise, and Adele had domain over Feline Frenzy. Amber Haws ran the volunteer programs, as well as did goat yoga. But Adele's husband, Carson took care of the goats in the Goat Grounds.

Sawyer and Jeri took care of the chickens, and Sawyer worked wherever Hudson needed him most. Dave got him a lot of the time in LlamaLand, and he really liked Sawyer. He and Jeri were off the ranch for a few days while they went down to a hospital in Los Angeles to pick up the baby boy they were adopting.

"I need someone out at the cemetery later this week," Hudson said, glancing between Dave and Gray.

"I'll do it," Dave said, because Gray couldn't go off on his own so soon. Not only that, but Dave loved going out to the remote cabin about an hour's ride from the epicenter of the ranch. He liked laying on his back as the stars came to life, and he liked walking through the pet cemetery and thinking about the people who'd buried their pets at Last Chance Ranch.

"I just need a report by Monday," he said. "I want at least two sections mapped."

"Yes, sir," Dave said, though Hudson hated being called sir. Maybe he shouldn't bark so many orders, the way Dave's military sergeants did, and he grinned at Hudson, who rolled his eyes.

"Gray, you'll be with the chickens until Sawyer and Jeri get back." Hudson looked down at the clipboard in his hand. "Karla will have lunch today, and Dave, Gramps wants you to bring your new dog by for a visit." Hudson looked up. "We're moving horses from pasture six to pasture three today, and then Dave, you're free to LlamaLand."

Dave nodded and pulled on a pair of leather gloves. "How many horses?"

"Sixteen." Hudson turned and hung the clipboard on the nail by the door before putting on his own gloves. "Where are you from, Gray?"

"Marietta," he said. "It's inland a bit. Nice place."

Dave listened with one ear, wondering when Sissy had been in Southern California, an hour from the beach. That didn't sound like her at all, but Dave supposed he didn't know who she was anymore. Nearly two decades had passed since their romance, and a keen sense of missing pounded through his bloodstream he wished wouldn't.

The only way he'd been able to get her out of his system was through work. He put his head down and got the job done, and that pushed Sissy into the recesses of his mind, where she belonged.

━━━━━━━

THAT EVENING, he showered all the llama and horse smells off his body and out of his hair. BrainyGirl had wanted to go out that night, and Dave didn't have other plans. It had taken her a couple of days to answer him, but he didn't mind. Their relationship was casual, easy. He'd learned she liked chocolate croissants and staying up late.

He was more of a morning person, but he would eat anything with chocolate in it—especially Adele's peanut butter bars. The woman was a genius in the kitchen, and in addition to hanging out with the goats and taking care of over sixty cats, she ran a social media foodie channel. He and the other cowboys were always more than happy to eat her leftovers, and Carson almost always had something with chocolate in it on the workbench in the hay barn.

Hudson had put a mini fridge out there too, and everyone knew if you needed a snack, you checked the hay barn before going home.

Dave certainly didn't have great food at home. His time in the Army and his many years as a bachelor meant he *could* cook for himself. He just didn't want to.

He dressed in clean jeans and a blue T-shirt with the word ARMY across the front in big, blocky letters. It would give him and BrainyGirl something to talk about.

Dave didn't normally have a problem making conversation, especially if the food was good.

She'd suggested Scooter's, an upscale bistro he'd eaten at several times over the past year or so. He liked their jalapeño poppers, and their clam chowder was the best in Pasadena. He'd agreed readily, because the service was fast and the place was always busy. That alone would make a bad date just fine, and if things were going well, he'd suggest a walk around the nearby Balboa Park.

BrainyGirl had said she'd be wearing a red sweater, but there wasn't a woman in the waiting area wearing anything of the sort. Had she gotten a table already? He was five minutes early, already regretting the choice of restaurants because of the pounding music.

He couldn't wait for the silence and tranquility of the outer cabin, the lazy day walking through the pet cemetery.

And that was when he realized his life had reached a new low. His idea of a good time was wandering through a pet cemetery?

Please let this date go well, he thought. While he didn't really want to settle down, the constant revolving door of women was getting tiring. His plan wasn't working anyway.

Sissy hadn't been jealous of any of his dates. She hadn't even seemed to care. And none of them had helped clear her from his head.

Maybe BrainyGirl will, he thought. He had a good

feeling about her, and he stepped up to the hostess station so he could see into the bistro better.

"Can I help you?" a woman asked, and he looked right into the eyes of a woman he'd been out with last year.

A trickle of embarrassment ran through him. "Hailey," he said. "I didn't know you worked here."

She smiled at him, but not in the flirtatious way that had prompted him to ask her out. "It's only been a couple of months. Let me guess—you're meeting someone."

"Yes," he said.

"What's her name?"

"Uh...BrainyGirl."

Hailey's eyes widened. "So you don't know her real name?" The incredulity in her voice caused a passing waitress to pause. "Kirsten, he's here for BrainyGirl."

The blonde looked down to Dave's boottips and back to his face. "You're kidding."

"I feel like I'm missing something," Dave said. "Is she here?" He stood taller than the women, but he couldn't see a flash of red anywhere.

"He doesn't know who she is," Hailey said.

"Which means she doesn't know who he is," Kirsten said. They seemed to have forgotten he stood there.

"Excuse me," he said, maybe with a little too much force. Both women startled and looked at him, almost like he was a ghost. "Is she here?"

The two women exchanged another glance, and then Kirsten said, "Yeah, she's here. I'll take you back."

Dave followed her, trying to riddle through what had just happened while simultaneously searching the restaurant for that red sweater. He finally saw it, in a booth in the back corner of the farthest room. It was literally the table with the longest walk in and out, but Dave didn't mind.

This woman had long, dark hair which curled softly over her shoulders. The sweater was definitely red, and it was sleeveless, revealing tan arms.

"Right there," Kirsten said, and Dave stepped past her, his heart beating too fast in his chest.

As if drawn by his approach, the woman turned to face him.

He froze, his pulse whacking him with the force of gravity. It actually hurt as it radiated through his body.

"Sissy?" he said.

The woman who'd been plaguing him for many long years slid to the end of the booth and stood up. She wore a mixture of emotions on her face, ranging from disgust to acceptance to...hope? That couldn't be right.

She folded her arms and asked, "You're CowboyDan?"

He couldn't even nod. All he could think was that God certainly had a sick sense of humor.

Or maybe He was simply trying to shove Dave into the place where he should be. It was a toss-up at this point, especially as Sissy continued to stand there and stare at him, no smile in sight.

Chapter Three

Sissy's heart felt like it would burst from her chest, and she'd be left standing there with a hole in her body.

CowboyDan was Dave.

And he hadn't run away yet. Hadn't rolled his eyes and headed for the exit. Could she get him to stay? Feeling so unlike herself, which honestly was what she needed to be, she said, "I sure enjoyed talking to you through the app."

His eyes widened, and Sissy glanced left and right to see almost everyone in the nearby vicinity looking at them. "Do you want to eat?" She turned back to the booth, praying with every fiber of her soul that when she sat and looked at him, he'd be walking toward her.

She sat. She looked.

He'd moved a few steps in her direction. Relief swept

through her in powerful waves, the way the ocean pounded into the cliffs in rocky areas.

"Do you really like this place?" he asked, his voice still in the rude category.

"I meet a lot of my blind dates here, yes," she said. "I know the waitresses here, and we watch out for each other."

One of the said waitresses—Clara—appeared at their table, her eyes a bit on the wide side. "How are you two? Drinks?"

"I want iced tea with a lot of lemon," Sissy said, looking at Dave. A smile sprang to her lips. "He wants Diet Mountain Dew with a lot of ice." At least he did eighteen years ago. And wow, eighteen years was a long, long time.

Clara gaped at Dave, who gave her a quick nod and ducked his head completely, obscuring his face behind that sexy cowboy hat.

Sissy really need to reign in her thoughts before she allowed them to get too far ahead of themselves.

Clara looked at her, the seconds lengthening, all kinds of questions in her eyes.

"We need a few minutes," Sissy said. "I don't think Dave here likes the food all that much."

"Yes, I do," Dave said, finally looking up as Clara walked away on somewhat wooden legs. Sissy had expressed to her girlfriends that she was extra nervous about tonight's date. She'd enjoyed her and CowboyDan's conversations so much, and she worried that they wouldn't hit it off. Or he'd be arrogant. Rude.

"You don't seem to like this place," she said, unfolding her napkin and laying it over her legs.

"They have the best clam chowder anywhere," he said. "It's just so...loud." He glanced around as if he could turn down the music with just his eyes.

"But it's fast," she said. "We could go somewhere quieter afterward." Why she'd suggested that, she didn't know.

Dave's dark eyes sparkled like black gold. He'd probably shaved that morning, but by this late in the day, he looked like he had a week's worth of growth on his face. She'd always been impressed by his scruff, and she distinctly remembered the feel of it beneath her fingers as she kissed him. The scratch of it along her neck as he kissed her.

Heat filled her whole body, and she cleared the thoughts from her mind.

"I like Balboa Park," he said with a small shrug. "Could take a walk there."

"Sure."

Clara returned with their drinks and tucked her hands into her apron. "Have you decided?"

Dave picked up the menu and put it back down. "I want the clam chowder and jalapeño poppers," he said. "And the surf and turf, medium-rare, please."

Clara didn't write a single thing down. She looked at

Sissy, and she had a feeling her phone would blow up before their dinner arrived. "I want the number four." She handed the menu to Clara, who gasped.

"Are you sure?" she asked, and Sissy grinned at her. She glanced at Dave as if to tell Clara not to ruin this for her, and then she nodded.

"I think there's something I'm missing," Dave said, picking up his menu again. He looked at the front and back of it. "There's no numbers on this thing."

Clara practically ripped it from his fingers and said, "Coming right up."

Sissy sighed, but she wasn't too terribly annoyed.

"What in the world is going on?" he asked. "They acted weird when I got here too."

"We're friends," she said again, unwrapping her straw and putting all of her attention on it to do it. "Maybe I've told them about you. And maybe I told them about CowboyDan."

Dave was a smart guy, and he started nodding before she finished speaking. "So they were worried about how you'd react when you found out I was CowboyDan."

"I'm assuming. I don't know what they did when you got here."

"They looked at me like I was a sea monster," he said. "Bigfoot. Loch Ness. That kind of thing."

She burst out laughing, because her friends could exhibit some major drama from time to time. He smiled and brought his soda closer to him too. "I like that laugh. I've missed hearing that."

Sissy froze, her eyes locked onto Dave's. More word vomit pooled in her throat. Could she be as honest with him? Almost like an out of body experience, she reached across the table and squeezed his hand. "I miss you too."

He stared at their hands, and she pulled hers back quickly, almost as if his skin had caught on fire. She had no idea what to say now, as she usually filled her first dates with stories of her life, her adventures around the globe, experiences she'd had.

But it was exactly those things that had taken her away from Dave. Surely he wouldn't want to hear about them.

"Tell me about your last tour," she said, clearing the emotion from her throat.

"Maybe after you tell me what the number four is."

Sissy couldn't help giggling again. "You really want to know?" She leaned into the table, feeling flirtatious. After all, this wasn't a stranger. This was David Merrill, the man she'd known so well for so long.

Yes, time had a way of changing a person. Experiences too. But down deep, he was the same, good man she'd fallen in love with. Could she survive losing him again? Maybe everything would be easier if he went back to ignoring her and she kept looking for someone on Christian Catch.

"Of course I want to know."

"Okay." She shook her hair back over her shoulders as

if gearing up for something difficult. "I come here a lot on dates."

"Yeah, I got that part," he said dryly.

"Hey, you've dated everyone with two X-chromosomes since we came to the ranch." She lifted her eyebrows as if to say, *So there*. And *Why are you doing that?*

"The number four." He took a long draw on his straw, and Sissy watched him, her throat turning so very dry.

"Yes," she said, blinking to keep her focus where it should be. "So we worked out a system. The number one means I need help getting out of this. Bring me my food quickly and don't let me linger."

"Ouch," he said.

"It's a scale of one to four." She didn't need to get into all the details. "A four means I like this guy and I'm having a great time. So don't rush. Don't worry. I'll call you all later."

A slow smile spread across Dave's face. Sissy worried that she'd said too much, too soon. That she was opening herself up to get her most vital organ sliced and diced—or that she'd do that to him again. She didn't want to be that woman. Didn't want to be deserving of the glares and the scoffs, the eyerolling and the animosity.

"I'm really sorry about what happened," she said, her voice quiet among all the hubbub in the bistro. She suddenly understood what he meant by this place being too loud. She didn't expand on what she meant, or when that something had happened.

Dave knew.

"Did you get to have your adventures?" he asked in an equally quiet voice.

"Yes."

Dave nodded, his smile fading completely. But he didn't look angry or annoyed. Just...handsome. Contemplative. "I'm glad."

AN HOUR LATER, they strolled through Balboa Park, the late spring sun starting to sink into the ocean in the distance. They'd talked most about the ranch during dinner, and she'd let him buy dessert just to make the date last longer.

"So I don't get to hear about the last tour," she said, not asking.

Dave took a breath in, held it for a beat, and then released it. "It was a very tough time for me," he said. "I'll save it for a different time." He glanced at her. "The first date doesn't feel like the time to tell the story."

Sissy smiled to herself. "So will there be a second date, Cowboy Dan?"

He chuckled and wiped his hand across his jaw. "I can't believe I'm going to say this, but yeah. I think I'd like to go out with you again."

"You don't go on a lot of second dates, do you?"

"So you *have* been watching me."

"We work on the same ranch," she said. "And it might be big acreage-wise, but trust me. The gossip circles are tight."

"Can I confess something?"

"Ooh, confessions on the first date." She nudged him with her shoulder, but he was so much bigger and wider than her that he barely moved.

He reached over and carefully, slowly—oh, so slowly—slipped his fingers between hers. "I went on all of those dates to make you jealous. Make you see what a great guy you missed out on."

Sissy turned her head and looked at him, holding hands and walking and staring at him difficult to do all at the same time. "Dave, I know what I missed out on."

He nodded, swallowed, and kept his eyes straight ahead. "Do you think we have another chance?" he asked, finally looking at her. "For real? Or are we kidding ourselves?"

She had absolutely no idea. So she told him that, thinking, *But if there's one person I'd like to navigate the second chance road with, it's him.*

Fear pinched her behind the heart, but she didn't let go of his hand. He took her back to the bistro, but she didn't get behind the wheel of her car. Darkness was falling, but there were still plenty of people eating.

Sissy didn't care. She needed to talk to all the girls about tonight, and she nodded to Hailey and Kirsten, and they'd get Clara. "Lots of Diet Coke," she said as she went past them, back to the corner booth.

Her stomach felt like someone had poured popping candy down her throat, and she didn't even try to suppress the happy sigh that leaked out of her mouth as she sat down.

"Girl," Kirsten said, only two steps behind her. "Start talking."

"Not until Clara gets here," Hailey said. "And she doesn't like it when you call her *girl*."

Sissy laughed, because no, she didn't. She was forty-three-years-old, for goodness sake. But tonight, she didn't think there was anything that could knock her off cloud nine.

Clara arrived a minute later, four glasses of dark brown soda in her hands. "I have ten minutes," she said, throwing down straws and sliding into the booth. "Talk fast."

Chapter Four

Dave woke the next morning with the feel of Sissy's hand in his. He had for quite a while after she'd broken up with him last time.

"Can this time really be different?" he asked, his eyes staring up at the ceiling. "And if not, why'd you let me connect with her on that app?"

God didn't answer him, and Dave got up and got ready for the day. There was always something that needed to be done on the ranch, rain or shine. Healthy or sick. Great first date or a bad one.

It was actually something that spoke to Dave's soul. He'd much rather be busy than idle, and the cowboy life was perfect for a man like him.

"C'mon, Stella," he said to his rescue dog. "Let's go see if Gramps has anything for you today." His pup came with him, but he easily outpaced the older animal. She was a mixed breed found on the streets in LA, and she had bad hips. But she panted along behind him, finally catching him when they reached the grass at the homestead.

"He's on the porch, girl. Go say hello." He lifted his hand in greeting to Gramps, who waved back. When he arrived on the porch, Stella was chomping on something Gramps had given her.

"Morning, Gramps," he said, sitting in the second chair on the porch. He didn't come every morning. Sometimes they only spoke a few words to each other before Dave went off to get his chores done.

Every evening, he found Stella on Gramps's porch, whether the old man was there or not. Sometimes Dave let Gramps keep her overnight.

"Mornin'," Gramps said.

"Good or bad today?" Dave asked.

"Pretty good." He stroked Stella absently, his eyes on the road in front of them, to the left, toward the entrance of the ranch. "Sawyer and Jeri are bringin' that baby home today."

In the afterglow of Dave's excellent date with Sissy the night before, he'd forgotten. "That's right. I'm supposed to put the balloons out." He started to stand up just as Gramps pointed.

"Carson's doin' it."

Dave settled back into his seat, a slip of guilt pulling through him. He'd told Scarlett he'd tie the blue balloons to the fenceposts at the entrance of the ranch and in

Prime's hand to welcome the new baby to Last Chance Ranch.

"Hasn't been a baby on this ranch in decades," Gramps said.

"Yeah," Dave said, because he didn't have anything else to say. Scarlett and Hudson had been married for a year, but he had no idea if they were planning to start or have a family. He was better friends with Carson, since Carson had joined the Last Chance Cowboys once he'd returned to the ranch last summer. He knew Adele and Carson were still talking about it.

Dave thought of Sissy. He was no expert in the ways of women, but he knew they couldn't have babies forever. When he'd dated her all those years ago, she hadn't been interested in marriage or family. She didn't want a house. A white picket fence. A cute backyard.

No, she'd wanted to travel. See the world. *Experience everything.*

He could distinctly remember the conversation they'd had about exactly that. Dave had thought they'd travel, visit, and *experience everything* together.

She'd broken up with him two months later.

Dave had made a few major decisions in his life since then, but he honestly felt lost most of the time. Adrift.

He sure did like Last Chance Ranch, though, and living out in the Cabin Community and sitting on Gramps's front porch in the mornings. He'd worked on three other ranches, staying no longer than five years at each place. He'd only been here for two, and he hoped he didn't feel like moving on in a few years.

"I better go help," he finally said, getting his old bones off of Gramps's porch. He wasn't surprised when Stella stayed behind and Gramps didn't say good-bye. He arrived at the robot mailbox, Prime, just as Carson lost one of the balloons in his hand.

"Dang it," he said, watching it float away. Dave laughed behind him, and Carson turned toward him. "There you are. Scarlett made me do your job." He grinned though, and he handed Dave the few balloons he had left. "Hold these."

Dave did as instructed, and they got each balloon tied in Prime's hand to welcome Sawyer, Jeri, and their new baby to the ranch.

"Once this baby gets here, nothing will get done on the ranch," Carson said. "So let's go get the basic feeding done so we can have the rest of the day off." He grinned at Dave, and Dave couldn't argue with his logic.

A couple of hours later, they had all the animals fed when the bell started ringing. He turned his head in the general direction of the homestead, where the bell hung from the front porch. He couldn't see it past the barns in the way, but he finished up with the potbellied pigs and wiped his hands down the front of his jeans.

Everyone would be going to see the baby as soon as they finished their tasks, and instead of going straight over to Sawyer's, he detoured toward the Administration

Annex. Maybe he'd see Sissy. They hadn't set an official time for their second date, but Dave had been thinking about it while he fed the pigs.

Several people streamed out of the volunteer building and adoption center. So many people Dave didn't even know them all. At least twenty volunteers, paid for by Forever Friends, came to the ranch every day to help with the animal care in the Canine Club and Feline Frenzy. Very few came out to the larger animal areas, which suited Dave just fine.

He didn't see Sissy, and he hoped he hadn't missed her. For some reason, he wanted to see her reaction to this baby. But the administration building had a west door, and she'd probably gone out that away.

He continued toward the east door anyway, and he heard Sissy's voice when he entered the building. He walked through the lobby to her office and found her on the phone. Their eyes met, and her voice trailed off.

Holding up both hands in a surrendering gesture, he backed up a few steps. She continued talking, ending her conversation several seconds later. She came out of the office, and Dave drank in the sight of her in that cute little black skirt and a white blouse with lemons all over it.

He grinned. "They rang the bell."

"I heard," she said, walking toward him in heels. Didn't she know she worked on a ranch? A living, breathing ranch, with almost two hundred animals on it?

33

He shook his head at her feet. "So I take it we'll be driving to Sawyer's."

She glanced down at her feet. "I can walk in these."

He bet she could and actually wanted to see her do it. "All right then." He gestured for her to go first out the door, which she did.

"That was Forever Friends," she said as they went down the steps. "They're doing an audit of our financial records." She gave a heavy sigh. "As if I don't already have enough to do, what with that new loan Scarlett wants."

"New loan for what?" Dave asked.

"Increased agriculture," she said. "From here out to the pet cemetery. Hay fields."

Dave slowed, his heart skipping a beat or two. "What about the cabin out there? Are they going to tear that down?"

"I don't know," she said. "Gray and Scarlett came by this morning and proposed a hundred and fifty new acres of alfalfa. And that takes cash to seed, cash to buy equipment to harvest, to plant, to water." She shook her head, her dark hair swinging wildly. She really could move fast in those heels and Dave sped up to keep up with her. "I'm obviously still working through everything. And now the audit."

"Sounds intense," he said.

"It is." Sissy slowed down and glanced at him. "So, Sawyer and Jeri adopted a little boy."

"Yeah," Dave said.

"Do you want kids?"

"Sweetheart, we haven't even been out on our second date yet." He cocked one eyebrow at her, wondering if she'd somehow seen into his mind, knew he'd wanted to be with her when she met the baby so he could somehow determine if *she* wanted children.

She pushed playfully against his bicep. "I know. I just...." She didn't continue, and Dave felt the melancholy nature of her words filter through him.

"You just what?" he asked, because he really wanted to know how she'd finish that sentence.

"Do you ever wonder if you've made poor life choices?"

He chuckled. "I think everyone feels like that at some point."

"Yeah." Their feet crunched over the dirt and rocks in the road. "I'm too old to have babies."

Dave didn't know what to say to the sadness in her voice. He reached over and took her hand in his, quite surprised she let him, what with all the potential witnesses. He realized in that moment that *he* was the one keeping them apart. He'd been the one to snub her, walk away from her at every ranch function, and go out with anyone willing to say yes.

Sissy had never said a word about it, and he wondered if he'd hurt her with his behavior.

Probably, he thought, humiliation filling him at how immature he'd been acting. Still, his heartbeat pulsed in the back of his throat, begging him not to let her shatter him again.

She released his hand as they passed the homestead, and they approached the crowd that had gathered on the front lawn at Sawyer and Jeri's.

Some people were leaving as Dave and Sissy arrived, a happy glow about them. Babies had a way of doing that, and Dave looked toward the porch, where several people sat. Scarlett and Hudson, Adele and Carson, Cache and Lance and Ames.

He moved toward them, not making a conscious effort to separate himself from Sissy but doing so nonetheless.

"What did they name him?" he asked the group on the steps.

"Brayden," Scarlett said. "He's beautiful." She sighed, pressing one hand over her heart as she gazed to where Sawyer and Jeri stood, still quite a few people gathered around them.

Dave waited with his friends, watching as Sissy got closer to the baby, Amber at her side. She looked nervous, but he couldn't really tell. He had a good memory, but he hadn't seen Sissy in so long that he wasn't sure what was nervous and what wasn't.

When it was her turn to say congratulations, Jeri actually passed the bundle to Sissy. Her whole face lit up, and she gazed down at that baby with pure love shining on her face.

Dave's heart expanded three sizes, and his emotions

spiraled up and out of control. He couldn't believe he'd been so stupid when he was younger. Couldn't believe he'd let her break up with him, walk out of his life, and get on a plane bound for Costa Rica. Couldn't believe he'd gone on his second tour to fight, instead of staying to fight for her. For them.

Half of him wondered if it would've even made a difference. The other half wanted her to look at their baby like that, adoration and happiness streaming from her.

She passed the baby to Amber, who likewise showered the baby with love and smiles.

"I'm going to ask her out," Lance said. "I have to." He stood up as if he'd go ask whoever he had his eye on right now.

"Who?" Cache asked, echoing Dave's thought.

"Amber," Lance said, lowering his voice.

Cache exchanged a glance with Dave. "Whoa, bro. I don't think that's a good idea."

"Why not?" Lance looked back and forth between Dave and Cache. They'd started the Last Chance Cowboys in Cache's living room, and they didn't have a lot of secrets between them. Except Lance's crush on the blonde woman who ran their volunteer center, apparently.

"She's dating that guy who cleans the dog enclosures," Cache said under his breath. Dave noticed Scarlett was leaning a little too close to them.

"She is?" Lance asked.

Dave coughed, and that was the end of the conversation. He'd gotten his answer about the babies too.

But he still had some questions about that cabin, and he turned to Scarlett and Hudson to get the answers he needed.

Chapter Five

I'll meet you at your place.

Sissy sent the text to Dave a few mornings later, their second date only twenty minutes away.

My place? he sent back. *You're at the ranch?*

She looked away from her phone and down at the peaceful, slumbering baby in her arms. This might be as close as she ever got to holding a gift straight from heaven, and Jeri had been kind enough to let her stop by before seven in the morning.

"Trust me," she'd said when Sissy had said she could say no. "We're up. If you'll hold him for half an hour, I can shower without panicking."

And so Sissy had been stopping by at six-forty-five for the last three days, snuggling with baby Brayden while Jeri got her shower, and then going to work to deal with the audit and the loan details.

The time she spent in the living room with that baby had quickly become the highlight of her entire life. And she hadn't even had to fly for twenty-four hours to get the experience.

Another wave of unrest rolled through her. She was really second-guessing herself and all the choices she'd made up to that point in her life. If she'd have known how much joy a newborn would bring her, she might not have been quite so hasty to break up with Dave. At the very least, she would've focused on different things in her life.

Can't change it, she thought. *Does no good to look backward.*

But rocking a baby was one of the most soothing things on the planet. She did that until she had three minutes to get to Dave's house. He'd said he could get a late start on the feeding in Piggy Paradise, and they were going to breakfast for their second date.

Jeri still hadn't come down the hall, and Sissy got up and padded that way, patting the baby as she went. "Jeri?" she asked, knocking lightly on the door. Brayden didn't stir even the tiniest bit, and Jeri didn't answer.

Sissy pushed the bedroom door in to find her fast asleep. Fondness for the woman struck Sissy right behind the heart, and she silently moved over to the bassinet beside the bed and carefully laid Brayden down.

He made a soft groaning noise, his tiny face scrunching for a moment. His eyes didn't open, and he settled right back to sleep.

Sissy tiptoed out, hoping he'd let his mom sleep for a while.

She grabbed her phone from the arm of the couch, realizing Dave had called her. She dialed him back, slipped on her heels, and hurried out the front door.

"Where are you?" he asked.

"Coming," she said, not ready to share her new morning routine with him. "Yes, I'm on the ranch already."

"You're working too hard on this loan," he said. "There's not a fire, sweetheart."

She felt like there was, and she didn't particularly like him telling her she didn't need to work so hard.

"I'm coming down your street now. Get in your big truck and come pick me up, cowboy."

He laughed, the sound carrying down the road to her ears and booming through her phone. "I'm hanging up now," she said, and she ended the call. He backed out of his driveway, and Sissy waited on the side of the road.

After she'd climbed into his truck, she wrestled with her skirt to get it to lay right. "This thing is huge," she complained. "How do you get in without a ladder?" She yanked the fabric out from under her and smoothed it down, feeling sweaty and out of sorts already and they hadn't even left the ranch yet.

"You didn't need to walk over from the Admin Annex," he said. "I would've come to get you." He cut her a look out of the side of his eye as they turned to leave the ranch.

Sissy drew in a deep breath, wondering how to tell him she wasn't in the Admin Annex. He obviously didn't see her car parked right there in Jeri's driveway. She put a smile on her face and said, "It's fine. It's going to be a beautiful day."

"That it is." He reached for her, but his monster truck really was huge. "Come sit by me."

"Are you kidding?" she asked with a heavy dose of teasing in her voice. "My skirt doesn't allow for sliding across seats."

His lips twitched with a smile. "Maybe you just don't want to hold my hand."

She did, but she didn't want to seem desperate to do it. "Fine," she said, making a big show of unbuckling her seat belt and gathering the little bit of fabric on the pencil skirt so she could make the move.

It happened, but it was awkward and difficult. She smoothed her skirt, making sure she wasn't showing too much leg, before he took her hand in his. He lifted her fingers to his lips and pressed them there.

Sissy's body reacted, almost violently. She hadn't realized how many dormant feelings she still harbored for Dave. Did he have some still-there feelings for her too? From eighteen years ago?

"I'm going to be heading out to the cabin this week," he said.

"Right. The pet cemetery thing." She squeezed his hand. "What did Scarlett and Hudson say about the cabin? Are they going to tear it down?"

"No," he said. "They're going to leave it, thankfully. When they send cowboys out there for harvesting and whatnot, it'll get used."

"Good," Sissy said, knowing Dave loved that cabin for some reason and hadn't wanted it removed to make room for alfalfa fields. Truth was, there was plenty of room at Last Chance Ranch for both. "Why do you like the cabin so much?"

"It's...nice to get away from time to time," he said.

"You live on a ranch no one in town even knows exists," she said. "What do you need to get away from?"

He looked at her, something raw and vulnerable in his eyes. "Things."

"Oh, I see. We're not saying."

"That's right," he said. "We're not saying. Yet."

He didn't trust her. The thought stung, because it was absolutely true. He wasn't going to share much of himself until he knew she wasn't going to rip out his heart and throw it as far as she could.

She suddenly felt like crying. Maybe she had done that before. She hadn't meat to, but maybe she had. "I'm sorry," she said very quietly.

"For what?"

"For last time," she said, the floodgates in her head about to open. "For making it so we couldn't be friends.

That you had to go out with so many people to try to prove you were over me. For—"

"I *am* over you," he said.

Sissy shook her head. This wasn't going well at all, and she had so much work to do, and she wanted to ask him to turn the truck around and take her back to Jeri's so she could hold Brayden again.

Her mind traveled back through time, to the first trip she'd taken after breaking up with him. "Years ago, I went to Costa Rica," she said, not really sure how long this story would be, or why she was telling him. Beside her, he stiffened, his grip becoming tight and painful until he released her hand completely.

She kept going anyway, folding her hands in her lap. "It was beautiful. We hiked to all these waterfalls. Went to the beach. Museums. Sampled food." She sighed with the memories. "I had a good time."

"I'm so happy for you," he said dryly, his fingers strangling the steering wheel.

"I could've had a great time," she said. "An amazing time." She looked at him, having the luxury to do so without having to glance away to keep the truck on the road. His jaw twitched, and she reached up and ran her hand down the side of his face, hoping to loosen it.

"I realized on that trip—which was the first one I took after we broke up—that I could've had a better time if you were there with me."

He glanced at her, his dark eyes almost slicing right

through her. "Sissy," he said. "I don't...." He sighed and didn't say anything else.

"I'm sorry," she said again. "I know I hurt you last time, and I just want you to know I'm sorry." She didn't know what else to say. She didn't want to imply he was weak and not over her, which he'd obviously interpreted her apology to mean.

He pulled into the parking lot at a diner Sissy loved and parked. Neither of them moved to get out; he didn't even take his hands off the wheel.

"My last tour was so difficult because I didn't have you waiting for me at home," he said, his voice as tight as the rest of him. "So yes, Sissy. You hurt me. But I really am okay now."

"I know that," she said. "And your beard grows just as fast now as it did then. And you're just as hard-working." She reached over and gently took one hand from the steering wheel. "Just as handsome."

That got him to look at her, and Sissy felt a measure of love for him. For this strong, caring man she'd once loved so deeply.

"So some things are the same," she said, her voice barely leaving her throat. "But I know so many others will be different. And I want to know about all the differences."

There. She'd said it. Apologized. Confessed her intense attraction and crush on the man. She hoped he could read through those lines as easily as he usually did.

Just to make sure, she stretched up and placed a long, lingering kiss on his cheek. Only pulling back an inch or so, she whispered, "And I'm starving. Can we go in now?"

LATER THAT DAY, Sissy left the Administration building when Dave texted her that he was leaving for the cabin. After the kiss, Dave had relaxed and breakfast had gone well. He shared a few stories about his life on the ranch so far, but he hadn't dipped into the pool of his past even once.

Sissy told herself to be patient. They needed time to come to terms with how things had ended last time, time to learn about each other as they were now.

The steady clip-clop of horse's hooves came toward her, and she turned toward the magnificent sight of Dave atop of pretty brown and white horse. He spoke to it and it stopped, allowing him to swing out of the saddle and come toward her.

He wore happiness in his eyes, and she grinned at him. "Leaving?"

"Yeah," he said, sweeping into her personal space and taking her right into his arms.

"Oh," she said in surprise, and he jumped right back.

"Sorry," he said quickly. "I just saw you there, and...."

"And what?" she asked. She hadn't remembered Dave as one who couldn't complete sentences.

"And I wanted to hold you," he whispered. "But we're probably not there yet."

That little, three-letter word brought sunshine to her soul. Yet. "No, we are," she said, feeling adventurous and brave, the way she'd been when she'd gone parasailing in Hawaii, and when she'd ridden the longest zipline in the world in Mexico. Well, at the time, it was the longest. A new one had opened up in the Middle East, but Sissy had no plans to travel there and ride it.

No, she wanted to stay right here on this remote piece of land and be held by Dave Merrill.

She stepped back into his arms, glad when he enveloped her into his embrace once more. He smelled like the open air, and animals, and leather, and musk. She breathed him in and held onto those broad shoulders.

"How long will you be gone?" she asked.

"Until Saturday," he whispered.

She nodded, and said, "I'm helping with goat yoga on Saturday." She swept a kiss across his face again. "Come find me when you get back."

Chapter Six

Come find me when you get back.

Dave had Sissy's voice on repeat in his head. She had no idea the power she still held over him, and while he hadn't liked it at first, he was starting to realize that he gave her that power.

He still liked her so much.

He was not in love with her. He knew that. He had moved on all those years ago, and while she'd stirred him all up again, it would take some time for him to fall for her again.

"Which is good," he said to Chestnut, his brown and white palomino he'd brought with him from his last ranch. "I mean, we aren't going to get married next week or anything."

Chestnut said nothing, but the question still hung in the air between them. *Who said anything about marriage?*

And *Will she marry you this time, Davy?*

Dave shook his head to get the horse's insane questions out of his mind. He'd never married after his relationship with Sissy had ended. In some ways, he'd moved on. In others, he really hadn't quite gotten over her.

No matter what, he had a long way to go before he could trust her. Before he could even start thinking about marriage and putting himself and his heart on the line like that again. She'd apologized, and that was nice to hear.

He'd hated hearing about her time in Costa Rica—until she'd said it would've been better with him there. But she hadn't called when she got back. She hadn't texted. She'd just booked the next trip. And then the next. And the next.

He knew. Number one, he wasn't stupid. Number two, they had shared friends. Number three, she joined social media almost at its inception, and she wasn't shy about posting pictures.

Dave hadn't checked them all the time. He wasn't that hung up on her.

"She wants to know about me," he said to Chestnut. "But I haven't told her anything." He'd been troubled about why he felt like he couldn't share his life with her, but he told himself to give the relationship time. Time to grow. Time to develop. Time to build trust.

Chestnut snuffled, and it almost sounded like he said, "Rubbish."

Dave chuckled. "Yeah, I should tell her something, right?"

Chestnut tossed his head, and Dave took that as a yes. "All right, boy. You get us to the cabin. I'll text Sissy." He reached into his back pocket and extracted his phone.

He'd start with something simple. Something she didn't know about him that wasn't a huge secret and that wouldn't cost him too much if they broke up when he got back to the ranch.

Although, the very idea of that had him hesitating again. "You're not going to break up," he told himself. They were barely dating as it was. So he'd held her hand and been out with her twice. He'd done that with several other women over the past year too. Sissy wasn't special.

Which was the biggest lie of all.

Dave sighed again and tipped his head toward heaven. "Help me," he prayed, almost begging God to give him some direction. A shove, even if it was off a cliff.

His phone buzzed—literally. Dave had set the text notification to a chainsaw buzzing sound that drove Cache up the wall.

Send me pictures of the cabin, Sissy had messaged, and Dave felt like he'd gotten that push. He'd felt it in the restaurant too.

I will, he texted her. *I thought maybe I'd tell you why I decided to become a cowboy.*

Ooh, intriguing.

Sissy had always been great at flirting, and Dave smiled at his phone as if she were there with him.

As you know, I dropped out of college to join the Army. Served a tour in Afghanistan and was going back for a second one when you broke my heart.

He stared at the words, wondering if she'd feel bad when she read them.

"Of course she will," he muttered, checking first to make sure Chestnut was still on course and then deleting off the last several words. He sent the text without the accusation and looked up again.

That second tour was one of the worst things he'd experienced, and he knew now that it had everything to do with Sissy's absence from his life.

When I got back the second time, my six years were up. I didn't want to continue, so I left the Army and joined the reserves. I still go up to Fort Irwin once a month, but I've never been deployed again.

"Thankfully," he said, remembering the long prayers where he'd begged God to send someone else. He'd seen enough war. Enough of the desert. Enough death. Mercifully, God had listened, and Dave hadn't had to suit up and ship out again.

So I needed something else to do. Accounting was boring, and I wanted to be outside. So I took a job hauling hay at a local farm. The rest is sort of history.

Several seconds passed before she said, *Fascinating. When did you get the cowboy hat?*

He smiled and tapped as quickly as he could. *When you're outside all day, you learn quickly that you need a hat. I got one the evening I started. That first sunburn was a killer, let me tell you.*

Now, he could work for hours in the sun and barely feel it. He'd learned to stay hydrated. Always have a pair of gloves in his back pocket. Never leave his hat home—oh, and have several backups, though most cowboys had a favorite hat they wore. He had two, actually. One for working and one for going out. His working hat was dark brown, and his dating hat was black.

Sissy sent back a smiley face emoji, and Dave picked up the story. *I've always loved animals, and I took to horses the most. I worked at that farm for five years before I moved over to a cattle ranch quite a bit north of here. Still in California though.*

You always have been a California boy, she sent back.

Dave scoffed. He hadn't been a boy for a long time. His knees and back testified of his age every time he woke up in the morning.

I was there for five years, he said, choosing to ignore the boy comment. *And I moved to a boarding stable for a few years, and now I'm here.*

What has been your favorite spot?

"This one," he said to Chestnut, who he'd bought from the owner of the boarding stable a year before he'd moved on. He loved the camaraderie at Last Chance Ranch. Loved that it was a rescue operation, with disabled animals or strays or abandoned pets that would die if Last Chance Ranch didn't take them in. Loved his band. Loved his cabin.

Loved that Sissy was just a short walk away.

Last Chance Ranch, he texted, noticing that Chestnut had slowed and was pulling to get his head down to the grasses out here on the open range.

He shoved his phone under his thigh and picked up the reins. "Come on, boy," he said. "You're letting yourself get distracted."

Dave was too, and he didn't go back to his phone until he reached the cabin and put Chestnut to graze in the small paddock behind the house.

When he looked at Sissy's texts again, she'd said, *I like it here too.* And *I'm glad you're here.*

Dave was too, and he sent another prayer of gratitude to the Lord before he went inside the cabin.

Not many people came out to this place, so it looked and smelled exactly like last time he was here. Maybe there was a bit more dust, as the California winds tended to kick up in the spring.

The cabin had four bedrooms that wrapped down one wall and part of the back one, in an L-shape. The front door opened up into a living area on his right, with a kitchen in the back left corner. A small mudroom where cowboys could kick off their boots sat in front of the back door, which led straight into the paddock. There were no shelters for the horses out here, and while the weather usually didn't warrant one, they'd had coyotes on the ranch before.

Dave determined he could build a little barn in the paddock, and then immediately dismissed the thought. He didn't have time or resources to do that. And if Scarlett wanted something built, she'd hire Jeri. But Jeri had just brought home baby Brayden, so Dave knew there'd be no barns getting built any time soon.

On his left, a hallway led to two bedrooms with a bathroom between them. Various cots and bunk beds filled the rooms, as if at one time several cowboys had come out here together. As far as Dave knew, he and Hudson were the only ones who came to this cabin now, and even Hudson had started assigning Dave to all the jobs that needed doing away from the epicenter of the ranch.

He drew in a big breath and turned to pick up his saddlebags. He unpacked his food and water for the next few days, glad for the tiny battery-powered fridge that was big enough to keep meat and cheese cold. Everything else was mostly packaged, and for a few days, Dave didn't mind.

But when he got back.... He pulled out his phone and said *So am I* to Sissy's text about her being glad he was there. Then he added, *I'll be starving when I get back on Saturday. Wanna take me to dinner?*

THE PET CEMETERY held so much intrigue for Dave. He loved walking among the trinkets and grave markers, the chimes and wildflowers that had sprung up in the bare patches of earth. Some had headstones with a first and last name, but most were homemade markers with just a single name.

Bear. Thompson. Yeti. Digger.

He could tell the cemetery had been sectioned the same way the ranch was. In the horse area, the grave markers were much farther apart, but in the cat section, they were closer together. Cats and dogs seemed to be the most popular type of animal buried here, and their graves began just behind the big stone marker to the cemetery that read Angel's Nest.

The stone had fallen at some point in time, and Dave had resurrected it. He was glad to see it still standing strong the next morning, and he trailed his fingers across the top of it as he entered the cemetery.

Hudson wanted two sections mapped, and Dave pulled out the notebook they'd been using for over a year now. The birds had been done, as had the reptiles. The horses, and the cats. Only about a third of the dogs had been drawn and labeled, and he decided he'd start there.

As much as he loved canines, he'd never had one of his own until he'd adopted Stella. He'd always thought it impractical, because he was never permanent somewhere, and he could be deployed at any moment.

But subconsciously, he'd decided to stay at Last

Chance Ranch for as long as they'd let him. And if he got deployed, he could leave Stella with Gramps until he got back. He'd had friends at other ranches, but nothing like what he had here. Cache had taken Stella that morning, and he'd take her to Gramps that evening. The old man loved sleeping with a dog curled up at his feet, and Dave never worried when he had to come on his overnight trips to the cabin.

In fact, they rejuvenated him.

"All right," he said to the graves. "Me and Sissy. What do you guys think?"

The only sound was the scratch of his pencil as he boxed in graves and put names on them. It was easy work, which allowed his mind to roam through other topics. Today, it was only a singular topic—Sissy.

Dave wasn't sure what the future held, but by the time he returned to the cabin for a sandwich and a bottle of water, he'd decided he did want a future with Sissy in it.

He checked his phone, all smiles when he saw her text. *Of course I'll take you to dinner.*

Maybe, just maybe, she wanted a future with him too.

Chapter Seven

Sissy had just taken her mother's famous sausage and potato casserole from the fridge to start heating it up when she heard the door open.

Dave was early.

He'd been stopping by the Administration Annex a few times a week to eat lunch with her, and she'd bragged about the casserole so much over the last few weeks that he'd finally asked her to make it.

She wasn't a great cook, but she could slice kielbasa and brown it, open a bag of shredded hashbrowns, and put the dish together. It was full of cheese and deliciousness, and she slid the plastic container in the microwave just as Dave came into the break room.

No one else worked in the building full-time, but occasionally a few people congregated to eat lunch together. Today, though, the room was empty. Dave's late lunch

59

schedule helped them see each other alone, and he smiled at her.

"Horseback riding still on for tomorrow?" he asked.

"Yep," she said, taking an unconscious step toward him, like she'd get another hug like the one he'd given her before heading out to the cabin. She froze, a trickle of fear still icing her lungs.

She'd been letting Dave dictate how fast this relationship went, thinking he'd be as quick as last time. But nope. He'd been taking things slowly, carefully, and while he held her hand and texted her almost non-stop while he wasn't working, he hadn't even leaned forward to try to kiss her.

She'd told him about a few of her trips. Her job at the only other ranch she'd worked at—a small, family operation that needed a full-time accountant to fix their books over the last thirty years. The horse training facility was just outside of Marietta, and he'd nodded like that meant something to him.

When she'd asked, he'd said, "No, that's just where you met Gray."

"Gray was a mistake," she'd said immediately.

Dave had taken her hand, and in one of their most tender moments since they'd started seeing each other again, he'd said, "Did you ever think that about me?"

She hadn't been able to speak, but she'd shook her head and he'd grinned at her.

But still no kiss.

She was actually a little surprised she thought about kissing him so much. It wasn't like it would be the first time.

"The free ride starts at ten," he said, touching her arm. "Are you listening to me?"

"Sorry." She cleared her thoughts and fantasies, focusing on the moment. "Yes. Free ride starts at ten."

"Don't wear heels," he said with a grin, glancing down the counter. "We're eating salad? I thought you brought that casserole."

"I did," she said, pointing to the microwave. "It's heating up." She collected the salad and a couple of plastic forks and took them to the closest table. "Soda in the fridge for you."

"Ah, you know me so well."

Sort of, she thought. She had learned more about him —the man he was now—but she certainly didn't know him as well as she'd like. The microwave beeped, and she returned to it, her heels clicking on the tile beneath her feet.

"So no heels," she said. "Jeans, I'm assuming. Cowgirl hat."

He turned toward her. "You're going to wear a cowgirl hat?"

"You told me a proper cowboy learns fast to wear a hat all the time."

He simply blinked at her. "Do you even own a cowgirl hat?"

"Yes," she said. "I made Kirsten and Clara go with me to buy it." She smiled at him in what she hoped was a coy, flirtatious way. "They said it's very cute."

He swallowed, and she nudged him on her way back to the table. "Stop staring and come eat."

He did, positioning himself right next to her, as he usually did. His knee pressed into hers, and she slid a fork toward him. "Sunscreen," he said. "Might want to bring some of that."

"I do goat yoga a lot," she said, though it didn't usually calm her the way it was supposed to. All of her eating out and rich, creamy casseroles also prevented her from losing any of the extra forty pounds she carried.

Or maybe that was the stress she inflicted on herself from working twelve hours a day. Dave hadn't said anything about her work habits again, and he'd sat with her in her office a couple of nights when she stayed until seven or eight to prepare paperwork for the following day's meetings or calls with the auditor.

Her stomach turned at the thought of Mike Doyle. The man didn't know how to smile, and he could see an errant decimal point from twenty feet away.

"What does goat yoga have to do with horseback riding?" Dave asked, forking up a bite of food. He put it in his mouth, and she saw the exact moment he tasted it. "Oh, wow," he said around the food. "This is fantastic."

"I told you."

"Yes, you did." He put another bite in his mouth.

"And goat yoga is outside," she said. "Sometimes I help with all the sessions, and one of them is in the middle of the day."

"And you've never worn a hat?"

"No, sir," she said, shaking her head with a giggle. She expected him to laugh too, but he didn't. She glanced at him and found him staring at her again. "What?"

"Sir?"

"I think you have a little gray hair," she teased. "You're definitely a *sir*."

"Gray hair?"

She laughed at the mortified look on his face. "I saw you take your cowboy hat off for a minute last time you came to lunch," she teased, stirring her own casserole. "Looked like you were a little silver on the sides." She looked at him, flirting shamelessly now. "I like a more mature man. Very sexy."

Dave put another bite of food in his mouth and considered her, a tactic he'd done a few times over their informal lunches together. Finally he said, "My second tour to Afghanistan was a real growing time for me."

Surprised by the sudden change in subject—especially to something serious—had her whiplashing around for a moment. "Oh," she finally said. "Tell me about it."

She ate while he talked, realizing that when he spoke about men she'd once known too that she'd lost a lot more than Dave when they'd broken up.

"I thought I'd never get the sand out of my hair," he said. "Your gray hair comment reminded me of it."

"So that's why you told me," she said. "I wondered how we got from me teasing you about your hair to your second deployment."

Dave watched her again, his expression serious. Maybe Sissy was worse at flirting than she thought. He obviously wasn't picking up any of her playful vibes that day, at the very least.

"No," he said. "I've been wanting to tell you about it." He took one of her hands in both of his. "I'm learning to trust you more, Sissy. It felt like the right time to tell you. So I did."

There was the Dave she remembered—the one who just said things how they were, even if they were serious or emotional.

"Thank you for telling me."

An edge entered his eyes. "I think you might have something to tell me, too."

"Do I?"

"Sometimes my mornings start awfully early," he said, slipping his hands away from hers and leaning back in his chair. "I've seen your car at Sawyer's house quite a few times."

Sissy's muscles seized, and she suddenly regretted eating all that casserole. She focused on her salad, pushing the lettuce around with the cucumbers. "Yeah," she said.

He waited, but Sissy hadn't worked out how to tell

him about the baby. Brayden was pinker than ever, and getting chubby cheeks and staying awake after feedings. She'd forever be grateful to Jeri for letting her have almost an hour with the baby each morning, but Jeri claimed that Sissy was doing her the favor.

"And?" Dave prompted. "That's all I get? Yeah?"

"I'm not cheating on you," she said.

Dave burst out laughing. "I know that, sweetheart. And you and Jeri...? I don't even know what you would be doing with Jeri. You two are like water and vinegar."

"We are not," she said, feeling her defenses rise. "I love Jeri. We get along great."

"I know." Dave softened as he sighed, leaning into the table. "That didn't come out right. What I meant was, you wear adorable little skirts and blouses made of fabric I can't even name. Jeri wears tank tops, and jeans, and tool belts." His eyebrows rose, his point made.

Sissy's heart pounded. "I'm there to hold—look after— the baby while Jeri gets ready in the morning."

He pulled in a breath and sat back again, his eyes almost wild. "The baby."

"Yeah," she said with a small shrug though this was a very big deal to her. "I really love that baby." A smile touched her soul and spread across her face, its accompanying dose of sadness hitting her right behind the lungs. "And I'll probably never have kids of my own, so that little baby is my morning therapy."

"Why wouldn't you be able to have kids?" he asked. "Jeri's as old as you."

"Well, they're very lucky," Sissy said. "And Dave, they *adopted* that baby. She didn't carry it and give birth to it."

Dave looked like she'd splashed ice water in his face. "I know that."

She peered at him. "You know women can't have kids forever, right?"

"Of course," he said, a blush crawling up his neck and into that delicious scruff on his face. "I did hear last week on the radio that fifty is the new forty, though. So, I mean, you've still got time."

"Fifty is the new forty? To have kids?" Sissy didn't believe that. Not everything someone said not the radio was true. But a seedling of hope entered her heart. She'd definitely look it up later.

"Yeah." Dave shrugged, meeting her eye again. "Did you—I didn't think you wanted kids. You wanted to explore the world. Fly everywhere. Climb the highest mountains."

Sissy picked up her dishes and took them over to the sink in the break room. "I know what I wanted."

He joined her, one hand slipping around her waist. "Are you saying what you want has changed?"

She looked up into his face, and he looked down at her. Time slowed in that moment, and she trusted him. He was being open and honest with her. She nodded. "Yes, Dave. What I want has changed."

Finally, he leaned toward her like he might kiss her. Instead, he pressed his cheek to hers and whispered, "And what do you want now?" A shower of shivers streamed down her spine, and she trembled in his arms.

"A house. The white picket fence. You know, the works."

"A husband?"

"Yes."

"Kids?" His breath cascaded across her earlobe, and if he didn't kiss her before he left, she might combust.

"Yes."

He slipped away, his phone buzzing out that annoying notification as it rang. "Good to know." He tipped his hat at her and backed away while lifting his phone to his ear. He grinned at her in a way that said he knew he'd left her weak in the knees and wanting.

"Hey, Boss," he said, finally turning and leaving the break room. Sissy sagged against the counter, her heart-beat tapping out a rhythm that was much too fast.

Chapter Eight

May arrived, and so did the first weekend of the month. That meant Dave had to spend his time at Fort Irwin instead of Last Chance Ranch. He normally didn't mind. Life on the base, in the trainings and the meetings, felt almost like getting out to the cabin. It was something that was only his, and he normally liked that.

Sissy had changed that. He wanted to spend all his free time with her, and he'd made a conscious effort not to over the past month since he'd shown up in that bistro to meet BrainyGirl.

They'd spent last Saturday horseback riding and adopting out horses to the public who came to their weekend free riding event. He'd started to open up a little bit about his past. She shared way more than him, but she'd only detailed a few of her trips.

His irritation with her skyrocketed when she started a story with, "So there was this one time I was in Mexico...."

Or Switzerland. Or they Himalayas. Or Japan. Australia. London.

Dave had only left the state of California to go to the Middle East, to fight a war. He sometimes felt so removed from Sissy and the life she'd had. Of course, he *was* removed from it. *She'd* removed him from it.

But now, she really seemed like she wanted something different. A house. The white picket fence. Kids. Husband.

All the things he wanted—except the yard work. He sure did like living on the ranch where Scarlett had someone come through and mow everything once a week. It was as much a fire hazard as anything, and Dave didn't weed or mulch or mow.

"Hey, there's the cowboy." Ben sat down beside him, his grin wide and perpetual. "How's life at Last Chance Ranch?"

"Good enough," Dave said. "You still with the cable company?"

"Unfortunately," Ben said, though Dave hadn't really thought he'd quit. He'd known Ben for years, and he'd hated his job with the cable company since day one. He threatened to quit every time Dave saw him, but he knew he never would.

They paid well, and they got all their services for half off. His wife couldn't give up that screaming fast

Internet or her three hundred channels, premium ones included.

"Starlee's pregnant again," Ben said, taking off his dress shoes and throwing them in his locker.

"Wow," Dave said. "Congrats, soldier."

Ben rolled his eyes. "Do you think four kids is too many?"

"Even if it is," Dave said. "What are you going to do about it now?"

"Good point." He sighed as he changed into his fatigues, spending just as much time as Dave did on lacing the boots just right.

"How old is Starlee?" he asked. Ben was the same age as him, though he didn't have any of the silver Sissy had accused Dave of having.

"Forty," he said. "She's freaking out a little."

"Why's that?" he asked.

"I guess there are increased risks when you have a baby in your forties," he said. "Genetic defects and things like that." He sighed as he combed his hair. "And we thought we were done. Sophie is six."

Dave nodded, noticing that Ben was carrying some extra stress too. He was probably freaking out a little too. "I'm sure it will work out," he said. "You'll love that baby when it comes."

He thought of Sissy going to Jeri and Sawyer's early in the morning to hold their baby. She loved Brayden, and he wasn't even hers. He'd seen and felt the love coming from her when she'd told him about the baby last week. Jeri and Sawyer loved Brayden unconditionally too.

"I'm sure we will," Ben said. "We better get in there. Sarge will filet us if we're late."

Dave agreed, and he followed Ben down the hall and into the conference room where they'd learn about their trainings and drills for that weekend. His mind didn't focus on the stratagem though. Instead, he let it wander down the road where he and Sissy had the nice, new house on the ranch. The picket fence. The newly adopted baby.

It was a nice picture, filled with joy and peace.

And he suddenly wanted it very, very badly.

Do we though? his heart asked—the section that still bled from the last time Sissy had carved it out and left it to beat all alone.

Yes, he told it. *Yes, we do.* He wasn't exactly sure, but he knew he didn't want to stay stuck in this holding pattern for much longer.

He didn't want to go much faster, and he was glad he'd taken some time to work through feelings he hadn't even known he had. He wanted to trust Sissy, and telling her about his loneliness and utter despair the last time he'd been overseas had lifted a burden from him that only she could carry.

As he sat down and tried to listen to his commanding officer, he wondered how many more burdens he carried, and how long it would take to get to a place where he thought he could trust Sissy wholeheartedly.

Of course, that would require that he had his whole heart to begin with, and he wasn't sure he did.

In fact, he was pretty certain she'd kept some pieces from last time and had already seized a couple of new ones this time.

He wasn't sure what that made him. Foolish? Desperate? Ridiculous?

Or just a man?

"Merrill," a man barked, and he flinched.

"Yes, sir," he said automatically, blinking out of his thoughts. He was definitely stupid for not paying attention to his sergeant during the briefing, and Ben kicked his foot.

Dave cut him a glance, and Ben chin-nodded toward the board, as if Dave should know what to do.

He had no clue, but the drawing on the board looked like a schematic he'd seen before. He stood slowly, trying to guess what Sergeant Sanders had asked him.

"Do you need me to repeat the question?" the Sarge barked.

"Yes, sir," Dave said.

Sanders got right in his face. "Whoever she is, Sergeant, she's not here this weekend. Got it?"

"Yes, sir," Dave said, already thinking about Sissy and how she'd said those exact words to him. He could admit that hearing her call him *sir* in her pretty little voice had gotten his blood heated in the best way possible.

But she wasn't here, and he needed to diffuse this bomb from memory.

73

SISSY'S CAR waited in front of his house when he returned to the ranch on Monday. As he pulled into his driveway, he watched her emerge from her vehicle with two pizza boxes. His soul sighed at the same time his mouth watered.

"Aren't you the best girlfriend ever?" he asked, ready to flirt with her after a grueling weekend in the heat, diffusing fake bombs and watching how far the explosive dogs had come in their training.

"Girlfriend?" She tripped in those heels on his uneven dirt driveway, and he threw out a hand to stead her. Or save the pizza. Honestly, he wasn't sure which.

"Well," he said with a shrug, not sure what else to say.

"I sort of thought you'd be in your uniform," she said, a pinch of disappointment in the lines around her eyes.

"Yeah?" he asked. "Well, I'm not. We change when we get there."

"Three nights away," she said, lifting the boxes. "I thought you might be hungry."

"You thought right." He led her toward his cabin, having a mild moment of panic as he thought about what condition he'd left it in.

Not too bad, as he didn't make much more than coffee and scrambled eggs. Sometimes he'd pour a bowl of cereal and stick something in the toaster oven. Appliances bigger than that scared him, and he didn't use the regular oven much.

He didn't keep his front door locked, and he led her inside. It didn't smell like dirty laundry or old food, so he figured he was safe to let her in. She glanced left and right as if the cabin itself would be impressive or big.

It was neither, but for Dave, living alone with his dog, it was just right.

"This is nice," she said. "I haven't been in one of these."

"In two years?" he asked. "You've never been inside one of these cabins?"

"I guess I came over for Jeri's wedding," she said. "But I don't live here, Dave. And I haven't been dating anyone else." She gave him a pointed look. "You never did clarify girlfriend."

"Nothing to clarify," he said. "I'm seeing you and no one else. That makes you my girlfriend." He sat on the couch and kicked off the pinching athletic shoes he wore to the base each month. "Does that bother you? The title?" He could call her something else if she wanted.

"You haven't kissed me." She kept her back to him as she spoke, and Dave couldn't judge how she felt about that.

He got up and approached her like he would a hurt animal. "And you want me to kiss you?"

"Duh," she said, finally turning to look at him. She wore her hair down today, and it fell in loose waves over her shoulders.

"Well, I don't know if that's obvious," he said. "I wasn't

75

sure." Of course he'd fantasized about kissing her again. His gaze dropped to her mouth right then, and the way his heart sprinted in his chest, he knew he wasn't ready.

Which sounded stupid, and another blast of foolishness hit him. What if he was never ready? Why couldn't he get over her?

In that moment, he realized he didn't need to get over her. He didn't really need to trust her. He needed to get over *what she'd done* to him. He needed to forgive her for what she'd done. Only then would his still-wailing heart be able to consider a real relationship with her.

He just wished he would've figured that out before calling her his girlfriend. Because what kind of jerk did that make him if he couldn't forgive her, couldn't kiss her, and had to break up with her?

"So not today," she said, putting a bright smile on her face. "All right." She faced the pizza boxes again. "I know it's been a while since I knew all of your favorites. But I'm hoping you still like...supreme with extra green peppers." She beamed at him for a moment, tucked her hair behind her ear, and opened the second box. "And garlic cheese twists."

His mouth watered, first at the sight of two of his favorite foods, and then at the sight of the beautiful woman who'd brought them to him.

"You nailed it," he said.

She giggled, and Dave sure did like the sound of that. He liked having her in his house. He liked spending time with her. He wanted to do more laughing, more hanging out, more of everything.

He'd missed church the day before, but he didn't have to wait to send up a plea to the Lord. *Help me forgive her,* he thought, wondering what that felt like, sounded like, looked like.

He wasn't sure, and that frustrated him. How would he know when he'd accomplished it?

"Oh my goodness," she said, her voice suddenly breathless. "You'll never guess what happened this weekend while you were gone."

"Yeah?" he asked, piling two slices of pizza on his plate and adding three cheese twists. "What?"

She took her food right to the couch, and Dave sure liked that she felt comfortable in his house. "Adele announced she was pregnant."

Chapter Nine

That night, Sissy lay in bed, the wrestle on Dave's face playing through her mind. It shouldn't be that hard for him to decide to kiss her or not. And yet, he seriously looked like he was trying to solve the world's hardest riddle—or diffuse a bomb, which the man actually knew how to do.

Foolishness pinched behind her closed eyes. Why couldn't she fall asleep? She was exhausted from getting up early every morning, all the girly talking she'd done that weekend. First, once the announcement had been made, she'd spent hours and hours in the homestead with all the other women, talking to Adele about everything.

Scarlett had participated, but Sissy had seen her wipe her eyes and disappear down the hall twice. She wasn't sure if anyone else had noticed, and she'd almost gone after the ranch owner the second time.

Adele was so happy she was glowing, and Sissy was happy for her too. Jealousy had poisoned her for several seconds—until she realized Adele was only eight months younger than her. And pregnant.

It was a high-risk pregnancy, of course, and Adele was taking all the precautions seriously.

Sissy couldn't even get her former fiancé to kiss her. Sure, he used all the right language. Exhibited all the signs that he liked her. But without that kiss, they might as well use the label *best friends* instead of *boyfriend*.

She exhaled heavily and rolled over, dislodging Cleopatra from her usual spot on Sissy's hip. The cat stretched and turned in a circle, this time curling into Sissy's shoulder. She didn't care. She liked sleeping with the cat, as it reminded her that she wasn't utterly alone, and she couldn't very well let her blue parakeet out. Birds weren't that cuddly anyway.

Sunday had been filled with scenarios proposed by Kirsten, Clara, and Hailey. It was actually Kirsten's idea to get the pizza and be waiting for Dave in his driveway when he got home from the base.

She was so sure that pizza was going to be her ticket for a kiss. Dave had enjoyed it, and he'd confirmed that at least his taste in food was the same. There was still something holding him back, and she wanted to know what it was and how to get rid of it.

Instead of asking him, she'd relayed all of the pregnancy drama to him and then walked with him over to LlamaLand, where he got to work.

Sissy was expecting to hear on the loan that week, and the audit was almost seventy percent finished as well. At least then she wouldn't be working ten or twelve hours a day, and maybe she'd have more time to spend with Dave.

But he didn't seem bothered by how much she worked now. He seemed fine with casual, and Sissy had seen him do that with over a dozen women over the past couple of years. Why had she thought it would be different with her?

"Because, it *is* different," she muttered to herself.

But maybe it wasn't. Maybe she was just another of Dave's women, though she'd never seen him go out with the same one more than twice. And never spread out over the course of a month.

She tossed again, and Cleo got up and jumped down from the bed, clearly perturbed about all the shifting. Sissy wanted to tell her to join the club, because all she wanted to do was fall asleep. Then at least she'd stop thinking about Dave.

And kissing Dave. Holding Dave's hand. Building a life with Dave. A life with pregnancy news and rocking chairs and diapers.

She remembered the sweet, sensual way he'd once held her face in both of his hands as he kissed her. And finally, finally, she fell asleep, sweet dreams accompanying her.

Sissy yawned while she went through another stack of files. Making physical copies of everything for Forever Friends should've been done from the beginning, but she was the first professional accountant the ranch had had.

And Gramps...wasn't exactly organized or detailed when it came to financial records. The audit had honestly been a nightmare, and the further she went back, the worse it became.

But she'd got to hold Brayden that morning, and Jeri had asked her to babysit that weekend. Sissy hadn't known what to say, so she'd said she'd check her schedule and let Jeri know.

Hours had passed, and her schedule was clear for Friday night, and she could easily babysit.

But she was afraid of being with the baby alone for that long. Why, she wasn't sure. But she didn't think she could sit in the rocker for hours while Jeri and Sawyer went to dinner and a movie.

She considered asking Dave out so she'd have a reason she couldn't help her friends, but she didn't want to be that person. She didn't lie about things.

Besides, she could still see that raging indecision in his eyes, and annoyance flowed through her. She placed paper after paper, making copies and organizing them into files. Forever Friends would get whatever she had, and she'd have to pray it was enough.

In fact, she sent up a prayer for exactly that, an idea popping into her head. She pulled out her phone and sent a couple of texts.

To Dave: *Want to sit by me in church on Sunday?*

To Jeri: *I'm free on Friday night.*

She swore she heard Jeri's squeal from all the way down the road, and her text came in almost immediately with a half a dozen exclamation points. Dave didn't answer, and Sissy went back to her files and copies. Copies and files.

Sometimes her job was extremely boring.

The week passed quickly as boring task after boring task piled up and helped the hours go by like water through her fingers. On Friday afternoon, she left early so she could go home and change out of her skirt and into her yoga pants.

Jeri had said she could sleep in the guest room so she could make it to seven o'clock goat yoga and not have to get up at the crack of dawn. She'd brought a small overnight bag of toiletries and a pair of pajamas, and she waited on the front porch while the doorbell rang inside the house.

Jeri opened the door with baby Brayden cradled in her arms. "I told you it would be Aunt Sissy," she cooed at the little boy. She passed Brayden to her, taking her bag and saying, "Come on in, Sissy."

The air smelled like lemons and peppermint inside, as well as the undertones of marinara sauce. "Sawyer put a frozen lasagna in the oven for you," she said, lifting her purse as her husband came into the kitchen.

"Hey, Sawyer," Sissy said, bouncing the baby and patting his bottom at the same time.

"Sissy," he said with a smile. "You ready, hon?" He stepped over to Jeri and pressed a kiss to her temple. She glanced from him to Sissy and back, her nerves plain on her face.

"I've got this," Sissy said, though a tremor of nerves squirreled through her at the thought of being left alone with the baby. Jeri was afraid to leave him, and Sissy was afraid to stay. She almost started laughing at the irony of it, and her smile must've convinced Jeri she could actually keep this tiny human alive for the next couple of hours.

Jeri stepped over to her and kissed Brayden's forehead, then turned and squared her shoulders. "Let's go, Sawyer. I can't wait to get a huge tub of popcorn at the movies."

Sissy suddenly wanted the same snack, with all its buttery, salty deliciousness. "Oh, we'll be fine, won't we?" she asked Brayden. He gazed up at her with his clear, blue eyes, and Sissy loved him so much.

Her phone chimed in her overnight bag, and she switched Brayden to her other arm so she could dig it out.

Whatcha doing tonight? Dave had texted.

He was asking her now? Sissy wanted to ignore him, and then a thrilling idea filled her mind. *Babysitting,* she tapped out with one hand of fingers. *Just down the street from you.*

She'd only had her boyfriend over while she'd babysat as a teenager, and they'd spent a couple of hours making out after the kids had gone to bed.

Could she dare to hope for the same tonight?

He didn't invite himself over the way Jexton had decades ago. So Sissy decided to pull the trigger and send the clearest signals she could.

Want to come hang out with me and a baby?

Of course, her intentions with Dave weren't a secret. She'd even told him she wanted him to kiss her, and he still hadn't.

"Maybe he just needs more time," she said to the baby. "Should we go sit on the steps and wait for him?" She nodded and bounce-stepped her way over to the front door. "Yes, we should."

She settled on the top step of the porch, the house directly across from the road where Dave lived. She didn't see him or his big, black truck coming, and she started humming to Brayden, her anxiety rising with each bar of music she sang.

"Should I ask him why he won't kiss me?" she asked the baby, and Brayden screwed up his face and gave a single wail.

"So that's a no," she said, putting the infant over her shoulder and patting his back now. He quieted again, and she couldn't believe she was taking her cues from a one-month-old.

Ten minutes passed and Sissy's hopes for her and

Dave withered with every second where Dave didn't show up and he didn't text.

She kept her eyes trained on that blasted road, almost wishing the quake of the century would happen, breaking up the smooth surface and giving Dave a good reason for not coming over.

"Hey," he said, and she jerked her attention to the right, where the sound of his voice had come from.

Just like that, the darkness in her soul lifted at the sight of Dave's five o'clock shadow and twinkling smile. "There you are," she said, her heartbeat bouncing as quickly as it ever had.

"Sorry," he said. "I was finishing up when I texted you, and then Cache grabbed me. We're doing band practice tonight." He grinned up at her from the bottom of the steps. "But I can come over after that."

The timer on the oven started beeping from inside the house, and Sissy stood up. "Yeah," she said, moving quickly down the steps and handing Brayden to him. "Let me grab that, and I'll come say good-bye."

Chapter Ten

Dave held Brayden like the baby was a yowling cat, his arms straight out in front of him. "Sissy," he said, but she dashed back up the steps with the speed of an Olympian. Brayden squirmed, and Dave didn't want to drop the baby, so he curled him into his elbow like a football.

He went up the steps and into the house to catch her setting a pan on top of the stove, the oven door open in front of her. The scene was so domestic and so surreal that he paused just inside the door. He'd imagined something like this between him and Sissy so many times, to have it playing out in front of him in live color made his heart jump around inside his chest.

He felt like he'd been put on a roller coaster a month ago, sometimes swelling higher and sometimes dipping so low, he wondered if he and Sissy could really have a future together. It probably wasn't fair for him to keep jerking her up and down with him, but he couldn't work out what to do.

"So church is still okay on Sunday?" she asked, discarding the pot holders on the counter beside the pan of lasagna.

"Yes," he said, smiling at her when she finally stopped moving and looked at him.

She cocked her hip and pressed it into the counter. "Well, look at you cowboy." Her eyes glittered like dark diamonds, flirting with him from a dozen feet away. She looked at the baby in his arms, and Dave did too.

He couldn't remember the last time he'd held a baby, and a sense of pure love filled him quicker than anything he'd ever experienced. She stepped toward him, and he moved toward her, easily passing the baby to her.

He gazed down at her, fear pounding through his whole system. His muscles felt weak and overused, because he'd been driving them to work hard this week. Anything to keep thoughts of Sissy dormant.

Without thinking, he swept his lips across her forehead and said, "I'll be back later," before turning and striding out the front door. The crack of it closing behind him made him flinch, but he didn't stop and he didn't go back.

He really needed to figure out how he felt about Sissy so he could stop giving off mixed signals, leading her on, and giving her small pieces of his heart every time he saw her.

"THAT END PART ISN'T RIGHT," Cache said, peering down at the sheet music on the makeshift stand in front of him. "What note are you playing, Dave?"

"E-flat," he said. "It would sound better if Sawyer were here." He wasn't sure why he had to be here, rehearsing songs they probably wouldn't ever play in public when Sawyer got to go out with his wife.

"Probably," Cache said, "But we started the band without Sawyer."

"Yeah," Dave said, glancing at Lance. He didn't seem to be bothered staying behind the drums on a Friday night. But all Dave could think about was the pretty brunette waiting for him down the road.

Seeing her with that baby had changed several things inside Dave. He felt like his heart was one of those slider puzzles, and pieces had been pushed and moved and suddenly clicked into place.

She'd been working at Last Chance Ranch as long as him. Most likely, she wasn't going to run off to the rain forest. To his knowledge, she hadn't taken a trip since starting at the ranch. Maybe that gypsy spirit really was out of her system.

And why did it matter if it wasn't? They could travel together.

Cache and Lance started playing, but Dave had no idea where they were.

"Dave," Cache said at the same time Lance started laughing.

"Sorry," Dave said.

"Dude, let's call it a night." Lance stood up. "I'm starving, and it's bonus burger night at Finer Diner." He surveyed the other two men in the room. "Who's in?"

"I'm in," Cache said quickly. Dave usually would be too, and it was no secret he'd been seeing Sissy.

"Me too." He lifted the guitar strap over his head and balanced the instrument in the stand near the front window. Sissy wasn't expecting him only twenty minutes after he'd left her, and he was hungry too. She'd pulled lasagna out of the oven, but when compared to a burger, the burger would always win.

"Really?" Lance asked. "Where's Sissy tonight?"

"Babysitting for Sawyer and Jeri," he said easily. "I have time for a burger." He looked at Cache and Lance, who both gaped at him. "What?"

"Nothing," Lance said, recovering first.

"Nothing?" Cache scoffed. "I think it's something."

"What is it?" Dave asked, truly confused.

"You want to hang out with us on a Friday night over your girlfriend." Lance exchanged a glance with Cache. "It's kind of weird."

"Oh, come on," Dave said, rolling his eyes. "You have an enormous crush on Amber, and yet, here you are, with us."

Lance opened his mouth to say something but snapped it shut. Dave looked at Cache. "And don't think I haven't seen you flirting with Karla in the stables."

"I have not," Cache said, puffing out his chest. "She likes Blade, and so do I." To his credit, he didn't blush or anything.

"Okay," Dave said. "But if I want to get a burger with my friends, I think I'm allowed."

"Yeah, sure," Lance said easily, the flush in his face fading.

Dave caught up to him. "I'm sorry I said that about Amber."

"It's fine. I know I'm obvious about how much I like her. And yet, she's still going out with that other guy."

"Just wait it out," Dave said, cutting a look at Cache, who was gathering his keys and wallet from the counter in the kitchen. "I mean, I went out with Amber a couple of times, and she doesn't take long to decide if she likes you or not. She'll break up with him soon." They went out onto the porch, and Dave drew in a big breath of fresh air. "And Cache and Karla are totally more than friends."

He glanced over his shoulder, a smile on his face. "They're really good at hiding it, though, I'll give them that."

He followed Lance down the steps and they all

crammed into the cab of Cache's truck. "So what is going on with you and Sissy?" Cache asked as they left the ranch.

"We're...seeing each other," Dave said evasively.

"Sounds like you don't know what you are." Cache looked at him and back at the road.

"I don't." Dave sighed. "We've dated before. In fact, I asked her to marry me once, a long time ago. We were engaged for just over a week."

"What?" Lance practically yelled at the same time Cache said, "You're kidding."

Dave shook his head. "It didn't end well, and I'm...." He knew what the problem was, but he didn't normally talk about his relationships with other cowboys. With anyone, really.

"I haven't forgiven her," he said simply. "So we're sort of stalled. It's fine. I'll figure it out." That was code for *I'm not going to answer any more questions*, and thankfully, the topic moved to something else.

Dave liked hanging out with Cache and Lance, and they had a great time at Finer Diner, which had live music on weekend evenings.

"I'm going to go see how we can perform here," Cache said after consuming his second hamburger.

"Cache," Lance said, but the other cowboy got up and left the booth anyway.

"He's a tyrant," Lance said darkly, and Dave chuckled.

"We should be playing somewhere," he said. "I mean, why else would we be practicing every weekend?"

"It's just for fun," Lance said.

"Yeah, but the Halloween carnival was fun last year," Dave said. "Right?" It was fun for Dave. As the lead singer, he'd gotten several phone numbers and several dates from the gig.

"Yeah," Lance said, his eye on a group of women across the diner.

"Which one do you like?" Dave asked.

"None of them," Lance said, blinking and looking away. "So how many more times do you think I need to go to goat yoga before Amber will know I'm interested?"

"Maybe just one more," Dave said, laughing behind the words.

"We're in," Cache said, returning to the booth. "Next weekend." His grin stretched as wide as the sky, and Dave watched Lance roll his eyes.

"All right," Dave said. "Let's go. I'm going to go hang out with Sissy now." He had Cache drop him off at Sawyer's house, and he knocked on the front door at the same time he opened it.

The living room and kitchen were empty, and he paused. "Sissy?" he called.

Footsteps pittered down the hall, and she wore a look of anxiety when she appeared. "Sh. I just got him to sleep." Her stage whisper was easily as loud as her speaking in a regular voice.

Dave touched his lips with his pointer finger and hooked his thumb over his shoulder. He turned and went back out onto the porch, encouraged when Sissy followed him, pulling the door almost all the way closed.

She left it open an inch or two and sat on the top step beside him, slipping her arm through his. A sigh passed through her lips, and they gazed into the darkening sky.

"So." She leaned her face against his bicep. "Are you going to tell me what's going on with you?"

"With me?" he repeated, his pulse tripping over itself the slightest bit.

"I'm not stupid, Dave."

"I don't think you are." And Dave knew exactly what she was getting at. "Look, I like you." He pressed his lips to the top of her head, feeling a sense of sweetness between them. "I like you a whole lot."

"Then what's the problem?"

Dave tried to find a nice way to put the words in the right order. He couldn't, and Sissy deserved an answer. "I haven't forgiven you yet," he whispered. "I'm trying, Sissy, honest I am."

Desperation rose in his throat. "I just need...I don't know what I need."

She put her other hand on his and squeezed. "I understand."

"I don't see how you can." Dave felt like an island, alone in a wide sea. He'd experienced this lonely, lost feeling before, and he didn't like it. He needed an anchor, something or someone to hold onto.

"Maybe I don't, then," Sissy said, throwing him a life preserver. "But I'm not leaving this time, Dave. If you need more time, it's yours. If you need me to apologize again, I will. If you need—"

"I just need time to work some things out," he said.

"Okay," she said.

"Okay," he repeated, sweeping another kiss along her hairline.

Now he just had to figure out how to forgive her before he lost her.

Again.

Chapter Eleven

S issy adjusted the necklace against her chest, making sure it laid exactly right. Dave should be arriving in minutes to get her, and she wanted every piece in place. Makeup. Jewelry. Clothes. Heels. Hair.

Checkedy check check.

She dressed up nice for work every day, but there was something special about taking a man to church. At least for her.

In fact, she'd only ever sat by three men in a pew at church, and one of them had been Dave. Out of all the men she'd gotten serious with over the years, Dave had the most faith. Gray hadn't wanted to go at all, but he'd obliged a few times and then said it just wasn't for him.

Sissy had known then there couldn't be anything lasting between them.

She felt the exact opposite about Dave, and when knocking sounded on the door, she jumped.

Pressing one palm over her now pounding pulse, she took in a deep breath and looked into her own eyes. "He's here," she whispered to her reflection, as if she'd never seen Dave before.

He'd confessed to her that he hadn't forgiven her yet. Though it had only been just over twenty-four hours since that confession, she'd probably prayed a dozen times for him to forgive her. For God to soften his heart and allow him to be able to see a future with her, right here at Last Chance Ranch.

"Sissy?" he called, and she left her bedroom and clicked her way down the hall to the living room.

"Hey," she said, putting a smile on her face. He looked great in gray slacks and a white shirt, a purple, blue, and black tie knotted perfectly at his neck. And that cowboy hat. It was different than the one he wore around the ranch, but she sure liked the deep, rich black color.

"Nice place," he said. "This is a cute neighborhood too."

"Cute," she said, grinning at him fully now. "And don't be too impressed. I pay a housekeeper and a gardener."

"Well, they do a great job." He kept his eyes on her as she moved closer to him. "Ready?"

"Yep."

He led her out to his truck, and she'd at least learned not to wear such a tight skirt when she needed to climb into the black behemoth of a vehicle. Today, she wore a long maxi dress with bright gold and yellow flowers on the black fabric. It allowed her to move and didn't have to be so perfectly positioned to keep her covered up.

She slid across the seat while he rounded the front of the truck, so when he got in, they sat thigh-to-thigh.

It was a short drive to the church at the bottom of the bluff where most of the cowboys attended, and Sissy held Dave's hand as they joined the people walking inside the building. She'd first come here because Scarlett had recommended it.

She'd stayed because Pastor Williams prepared great messages that spoke to her soul more often than not.

Her thoughts felt a little scattered today, though, especially when she caught sight of a group of women loitering in the lobby. Sissy didn't know them personally, but she and her girlfriends at Scooter's had kept track of everyone Dave had been out with.

And he'd been out with all four of them.

"Ladies," he said, tipping his hat at them as he went past, seemingly without a care in the world. Her smile, however, slipped and disappeared under the weight of the glaring.

"Hostile," she whispered to Dave once they'd made it several feet past the women.

"Oh, it's just Thea," he whispered back. "She liked me more than I liked her."

"I think they all did," she whispered.

"Nah." He dipped his mouth closer to her ear. "Margaret said no when I asked her out for the second time."

"Really?" She twisted further into him, and he lifted his arm over her shoulders. "Then why did she spear me with that nasty look?"

"She's Thea's best friend."

"And you dated both of them." Sissy shook her head, trying not to smile. She knew why he'd gone out with so many people, and she actually liked that he'd tried to find someone to replace her and had failed.

"'Dated' is too strong of a word," he said. "I went out with Margaret once. And Lizzie once. And Sara—we didn't even go out. I talked to her at the carnival last year and we rode the Ferris wheel together."

"Totally a date," Sissy said, focusing on the choir as they came out in their emerald green robes.

"You think so?"

"Did you buy her something? A drink or a funnel cake or something?"

"Yeah, popcorn and lemonade."

"Date," Sissy said, enjoying this whispered game of back and forth.

"Huh," he said. "I had no idea."

"She probably wanted you to ask her out again, and you didn't, so she's upset about that."

"Wrong," he said, sending chills racing across her skin from his breath. "I *did* ask her out, and she said no. If anyone should be giving someone crusty glares, it's me, to them."

"Good job for taking the higher road."

Dave chuckled then, burying his face in her hair. Sissy sat very still and straight, attraction sparking through her like a live wire. She smiled and nudged him when the choir began belting out their rendition of *Joy to the World*.

"Oh, geez," Dave muttered. "Someone needs to tell Julianne that it's not Christmas anymore."

"I like it," Sissy said, standing up with everyone else in the congregation. "It's very festive."

Dave stood beside her, silent, with his hands tucked in the pockets of those slacks. Wow, he was handsome when he wasn't wearing jeans. Handsome when he was. Always so handsome.

Please help him forgive me, she prayed again, an extra burst of gladness hopping through her when Pastor Williams stood behind the microphone and said, "Wasn't that a great song? It's always good to be reminded of the birth of the Savior who we emulate. One thing Jesus was very good at, and that we need to get good at, is forgiveness."

AFTER CHURCH, Sissy wanted to burst, the words in her throat threatening to come out all at once. But she wanted Dave to bring up the subject and say what he thought first.

So she sat on her hands all the way back to her house and let him help her down from his truck.

He kept his hands on her waist, his head tipped down within kissing distance. His big black hat would even conceal them from any nosy neighbors who might be watching. The reason her neighborhood was so cute was because the average age was fifty-five.

The women here loved tending to their lawns and flowerbeds, making bread, and visiting impromptu-style in the street after work.

Sissy loved it, but she couldn't believe she was thinking about her neighborhood while gazing up into Dave's eyes.

"What did you think of that?" he asked.

"It was great," she said, smiling. "What about you?"

"It's a lot to think about." He dropped his hands and fell back a step. "Easier to say than actually do." He waited for her to move out of the doorway, and then he closed the truck door and laced his fingers through hers again.

He didn't seem to have anything else to say, and Sissy sobered too. They walked up the sidewalk to her front door, and she bent to retrieve a loaf of bread wrapped in a brown bag. "Bread." Her voice held pure delight as she looked up and down the street.

No one appeared to take credit for the bread, but she knew who'd made it. Janis Gunderson, the little old lady who lived three houses down. It had probably taken her thirty minutes to walk down the street and back, and Sissy made a mental note to be sure to thank her later.

She tucked the bread under her arm and led Dave inside, the scent of the pork roast she'd put in the slow cooker before church filling the house.

"Lunch will just be a few minutes," she said, moving into the kitchen. She didn't particularly enjoy cooking, but she could put a decent meal together. Protein. Carb. Vegetable. If one of those came from a bag or a can, so be it.

And now she had the homemade bread, so lunch would be a huge success. She got the pot of water boiling for the potatoes and she opened the two cans of creamed corn and added one of regular niblets too. Butter, salt, sour cream, and the creamed corn was almost homemade.

Dave sat at her bar, his gaze somewhere besides the room. She peeled potatoes in the silence, wishing she had something wise to tell him. Wishing he'd gotten the answer he needed.

He'd asked for time, and Sissy didn't want to steal that from him. Eventually, lunch was ready, and she lined everything up on the counter in front of him. "Pork," she said as if he couldn't identify the meat. "You can make a sandwich out of it, if you want. Janis is amazing in the kitchen." She indicated the bread. "Creamed corn. Mashed potatoes." She looked at the food, thinking her mother would be proud.

Her mom and dad had divorced when Sissy was

fifteen and still had two sisters to take care of. She'd had to help a lot at home, and she'd often wondered if that was why she'd freaked out when she and Dave had gotten engaged. Like maybe she felt robbed of a few years of innocence and no responsibility, and she wanted to experience the world before she had to be responsible again.

No matter what, her relationship with her mother had been strained since then, because she'd loved Dave and didn't understand why Sissy was willing to give him up so she could go sailing and scuba diving.

Sissy didn't want to regret everything she'd done over the years, so she pushed the thoughts away and looked at Dave. He watched her, and she realized he must've asked her something.

"Did you say something?"

"Yeah," he said. "You were thinking hard about something."

"It was nothing." She didn't want to get into her mommy issues right now. Dave wouldn't know about them, as her mom had been antagonistic toward Sissy's life choices after he'd been cut from the picture.

"Let's eat," she said. "You still like meat, right?"

He chuckled, got up, and came around the bar. "I still like meat, yes." Dave swept his arms around her, bringing her close to his chest, right against his heartbeat.

Sissy tried not to melt right into him. Tried, and failed. He was everything she'd ever wanted—she just hadn't realized it until very recently. A sense of helplessness filled her, and she swallowed against her emotions.

She wouldn't cry because he wasn't ready to take the next step. Last time, they'd always been on the same page. Taken the same steps at the same time.

This time, all she seemed to be able to think about was that baby in the house at the entrance of the ranch, and how loud her biological clock was ticking. She'd never spent any time as a teenager fantasizing about her wedding, and the moment Dave said he loved her, she'd marry him.

Fear gripped her heart and squeezed—hard. She wasn't in love with Dave. Was she? Yes, she liked him a whole lot, as he'd said. She wanted to kiss him. But marriage?

Gotta be married to have babies, she thought. Of course, she knew some people didn't, but she also knew that her values were the same as Dave's, and they'd need to be married before they had a baby.

"Hey," he said, his husky, tender voice reaching into her thoughts and drawing her out. "What's going on today?"

"Nothing." She reached for a plate, her arms getting a bit tangled with his.

"I've asked you a question, and you didn't answer. Again." He took the plate and set it back down. "Talk to me. What's on your mind?"

Sissy swallowed, holding back the only thing she'd

been thinking about for a while now—besides kissing Dave.

"Babies," she blurted, thinking of the article she'd read that confirmed it was just as safe to birth at baby at fifty as forty. "I'm thinking about how much I want to have a baby."

Chapter Twelve

Dave had no idea what to say. He wasn't sure if he'd forgiven Sissy all the way, though the sermon today, with her hand tucked neatly into his, had helped. He'd seen her with the baby, and he decided on the spot that he didn't need to have every duck in the row. Every detail worked out.

He took her in his arms again and hoped she was paying attention now. Because he was going to kiss her. She realized it just in time to take in a deep breath, and then his lips brushed hers, experimenting, testing.

She tasted like butter, as if she'd tasted the corn or the mashed potatoes before setting them on the table. A moan started somewhere in the back of his stomach, because kissing her was still the most wonderful thing in the whole world.

He moved his hands to her face, wanting to experience her with every sense as she continued to kiss him back.

He wasn't sure how long he stood there kissing her, but she eventually ducked her head and broke their connection. Dave kept his eyes closed as he steadied his breathing, listening to her breathe in and out, in and out.

"Sorry," he whispered. "For taking so long to do that." He stepped back and wiped his palms down the front of his slacks. "This looks great."

Sissy still said nothing as she picked up her plate and started putting food on it.

"That's it?" he asked, wondering if he'd forgotten how to kiss a woman properly.

Sissy set her plate down slowly and faced him. Her dark eyes blazed with fire and passion, and she stretched up and kissed him again.

Maybe he hadn't forgotten how. She certainly kissed him like she liked him, and Dave let her take the lead this time.

She pulled away much sooner than he did and touched her forehead to his. "Thank you."

He didn't like that she was thanking him for kissing her, but he wasn't sure why it bothered him so much. "Why?" he asked.

"I'm assuming you found some way to forgive me."

"Getting there," he said, picking up his own plate and grabbing a slice of that homemade bread. "So you're thinking about having a baby."

"Yeah," she said, focusing on the food. "I mean, I sort of told you that already. We've talked about how I want the house, the husband, the family."

"Well, yeah," he said. "I guess I just didn't realize you wanted it all right now."

"I told you I was getting older to be having children."

"Yeah, but then Adele got pregnant...." He let the words hang there, not quite sure why he'd thought Sissy could have babies too. But he did see the hope shining in her face, and he felt the feather-light wings lift him up too.

"Yeah," she said. "But it's fine. I mean, we've only been dating for a month."

"I knew after a month last time," he said, and Sissy jerked her attention to him, slopping creamed corn over the edge of her plate.

"What?"

Dave chuckled, but it held a hint of darkness in the undercurrent. "I knew after a month last time," he said again. They both knew how last time had worked out, and his heart begged him not to kiss Sissy again, not to risk everything for this woman all over again.

He followed her to the tiny table in the corner of the kitchen, sure his knees wouldn't fit underneath. But they did, and Sissy poured barbecue sauce over her pork and buttered her bread. The silence between them was comfortable, unlike the past half hour while he spoke to himself and Sissy remained inside her own thoughts.

Dave still thought they had plenty to work out and

discuss, but he was enjoying the reduced tension between them. And the pulled pork. And that bread.... "This is so good," he said.

Sissy giggled and nodded as she took another bite of her bread. After she swallowed, she said, "We should go tell Janis how much we liked it after lunch."

Dave had a few other ideas for things they could do after lunch too, but he just smiled and agreed. The conversation turned easy after that, and Dave ate a lot and laughed loudly. After they finished, he did get his kiss and then they walked hand-in-hand down the street to thank Janis for the best bread he'd ever eaten.

MAY PASSED QUICKLY, with multiple days of record heat, horseback rides, dinners at Sissy's, and kissing.

Dave liked how this relationship was going, and while he wasn't ready for diamonds or diapers yet, he could see himself getting there fairly quickly if he could let go of his fear and accept the full sphere of forgiveness.

He liked eating lunch with Sissy and holding her hand during church. He liked walking with her in the evening, though it was like the devil had decided to heat the Earth himself. Stella waddled along with them as far as she could, and then she laid down in a patch of shade somewhere and waited for them to come back.

Summer had officially arrived, and he spent a week

shearing the llamas under his care. He sold the wool to his contact in Santa Monica and presented Scarlett with the wad of cash.

"You keep it, Dave," she said without even getting up from the dining room table. Dave stood there, staring at her. She'd never let him keep the llama wool money before.

"Why?" he asked.

Scarlett shook her head, tears splashing her cheeks. Dave glanced around, expecting Hudson to appear and make everything all right.

"What's wrong?" he asked. "Where's Hudson?"

"He went to see his mother." Scarlett wiped her face. "I'm so sorry, Dave. I'm just—we found out I can't have kids." Fresh tears leaked down her face, and she shook her head again. "It's okay. Hudson will be home soon."

Dave didn't know what to do. He glanced to the front door and back to Scarlett. "Should I have Sissy come over?"

"No," Scarlett said with conviction. "No, I don't want a pity party."

"It wouldn't be—"

She glared at him and shook her head so forcefully that Dave stopped talking. He couldn't just walk out, so he strode past the table and leaned down and hugged her. He probably smelled bad from sweating in the sun, but Scarlett hung onto his shoulders and cried.

Dave's heart ached and ached, and he wished there

was something he could do. The only thing that came to mind was to pray, so he did that.

He had the distinct impression that he shouldn't leave Scarlett here alone, and if she didn't want Sissy, she'd be stuck with him. He pulled out the chair kitty corner from her, and sat down.

Maybe if he got her talking, she'd stop crying. Dave had experienced his fair share of weeping women in the past, and it was hard for him every time. He didn't like seeing people hurt, and he wanted to help in any way he could.

"What's Hudson doing at his mother's? Don't they own a boarding stable?"

"Yes." Scarlett took a big breath and nodded, wiping her eyes. "She said she has an oil or something to help me feel better."

Dave wanted to scoff, but he held it back. "You sound doubtful."

"There isn't a water, or an oil, or a pill that can make me younger," she said. She glanced at Dave. "It's fine, honestly. Jeri and Sawyer adopted. If Hudson and I want children, there are ways we can be parents."

Dave covered Scarlett's hand with his. "You'd be great parents."

"Thank you, Dave." She flashed him a sad smile, and Dave couldn't quite comprehend how she was feeling. Sure, he wanted to be a dad too, but he knew it was different for women.

"I feel like a failure," Scarlett said.

"Scarlett," he said. "That's not true."

"I know it's not." She tapped her temple. "Up here." She put one palm over her heart. "But down here, I feel like I'm malfunctioning."

A steady of stream of sympathy filled him, but he had no idea what to say. "Where's Adele?" he asked.

"I can't be around her right now," Scarlett said, fresh tears appearing. "I know that makes me a bad person. I'm trying. I've prayed not to be so jealous of her. It's just so hard right now."

"Of course it is," Dave said, deciding he just needed to talk. "Did you know Sissy and I were engaged once?"

Her eyes flew to his. "No."

"Well, we were. A long, long time ago. Feels like a lifetime ago." He chuckled, though he didn't like laughing about this situation. "When I saw her here on the ranch, I almost quit."

"I'm sorry," Scarlett said. "I didn't know."

"Wasn't your fault. And I loved this ranch, so I stayed. I started dating everyone *except* Sissy, hoping I'd find someone else. Hoping she'd get jealous and realize how much she missed me." He shook his head at his own stupidity. "None of that worked."

"You're seeing her now, though."

Dave thought of the kisses they'd shared, the history they'd told to each other, how wonderful the past month had been. "I am. But it's still not all roses and chocolates. I'm...working on forgiving her."

Scarlett's eyebrows went up, but at least her tears had dried up.

"She was so hard for me to be around," he said. "Honestly, sometimes she still is. I want to shake her and ask her why she broke up with me all those years ago. I want to ask her if all of her trips and hiking and ziplining and experiences were worth it." He didn't like the bitterness in his voice. Didn't like the swirling, furious emotions in his gut. He forced a laugh out of his mouth. "I guess it's not the same as you and Adele."

She squeezed his hand. "It's close enough." She cocked her head. "You're in love with Sissy."

"No," he said. "No, I'm not." Not yet.

"Maybe when you let go of that last little bit of anger and hurt, then." Scarlett gave him a watery smile.

"Maybe," Dave said, leaning closer. "Do you know how I can do that?"

The front door opened, and Hudson walked in. His eyes were anxious as he immediately looked toward the dining room. He strode that way, and Scarlett squeezed Dave's hand one more time and got up to hug her husband.

"Dave," Hudson said. "Thanks for watching over her for me." He slung his arm around Scarlett and bent his head toward her as they walked out of the dining room.

Dave stayed for a few minutes, enjoying the air conditioning before he had to go back outside. Scarlett hadn't answered him, and he suspected she didn't know how he could let go of that anger and hurt.

He suspected it was probably different for every person. "Help me," he whispered to the ceiling, and then he headed over to Piggy Paradise, where the sheep had been gathered for shearing.

He held them while Gray and Ames got the wool off, glancing away when they nicked a sheep and blood appeared. He wasn't particularly squeamish, but his heart felt extra large that day, and he wasn't sure he could handle any animal suffering needlessly.

Dirty, tired, and sweating, he finally finished for the day. His phone sat in the barn, and he grabbed it on his way out. Sissy had texted several times.

Dinner at my place tonight?

You must be busy.

Watching you wrangle those sheep is super sexy.

Call me when you're done.

He smiled at her messages, and he definitely wanted her beside him after a day like today. So he called her, hoping she'd make that chicken cordon bleu lasagna if he asked.

Chapter Thirteen

Sissy took off the green tank top she'd put on an hour ago, suddenly unsure about it. Dave would be here any minute, and she had no idea what to wear.

She wasn't sure why she was so nervous to have him come for dinner. They'd seen each other every day for months, and he probably wouldn't have any clue that she'd worn the same tank top to lunch with him a few weekends ago.

But Sissy knew.

She'd just slid the meal he'd requested into the oven five minutes ago, and now she needed a new shirt. The doorbell rang, and she dashed over to the bedroom door and closed it.

Dave would just come in. He never waited for her to answer the door, and sure enough, his voice called, "Sissy?"

"Be right out," she yelled over her shoulder before ducking back into the tiny walk-in closet. She hadn't realized she wanted one that would hold three dozen pairs of shoes, all her clothes, and all of Dave's too—until she'd babysat for Jeri and Sawyer.

They seemed to have everything she now wanted and hadn't even known it. Even this house was too small for her now.

She wasn't sure what that said about her. She'd lived in a tent for weeks in Chile, and she'd given up her apartment for a three-month walkabout in Europe. Her home had never meant all that much to her.

She'd blazed her own way in the world, but now.... Now she wanted some stability. She wanted someone to come home to.

Knocking sounded on her door, and she realized she'd slipped into her own thoughts. She grabbed a light blue sweater and pulled it over her head. She hurried over to the door and yanked it open. Too late, she realized it was a cropped sweater, and the waistband of her jeans and a strip of her stomach was clearly visible.

Dave stared at the spot, reaching for her a moment later. "You look great." He kissed her, his hands electric on the bare skin of her back. She'd kissed him like this before, but it somehow felt different, and she ducked her head a moment later.

"Dinner will be a while," she said. "I just got it in the oven a few minutes ago."

"No problem." He grinned at her easily, sobering quickly. "You okay in here?"

"I'm still deciding on my wardrobe." She felt like the sweater belonged on a much younger woman, who wasn't carrying quite so many extra pounds. "I'll be out in a minute."

He backed up one step, then another. "Okay." He turned and walked away, muttering something to himself under his breath.

Sissy wasn't sure what that was about, but she closed the door and found a suitable replacement for the blue sweater. She couldn't wear a sweater in June anyway, not even a crop-top one.

With a sensible, flowery pink blouse on, she went out to the kitchen and living area of the house. Dave had kicked off his boots and lay on the couch, fast asleep.

She giggled to herself and set about making a green salad to go with the cheesy, rich dish he'd wanted.

"Sissy?" he asked a moment later, his voice quiet and somewhat slurred.

"Yeah?"

"You want kids of your own, right?"

She glanced at him, wondering why he was bringing this up again. "Yes."

"Scarlett can't have kids." He didn't open his eyes.

Fear struck her right between her ribs—all of them. "What? How do you know that?"

"I took her the money from the llama wool this morning, and she was crying."

"Oh, no." Sissy stood very still in the kitchen, her knife hovering above the cucumber she'd been about to slice. Emotions and thoughts tumbled through her, and she didn't know where to focus. What to say.

One thought became louder than the rest.

Scarlett is younger than you.

And she was. Sissy had been holding onto a false hope after reading the article about women having babies later and later in life. All she could do was stand there and watch everything she now wanted crash down around her. Despair gathered in the back of her throat, and she spun away from Dave's prone form on the couch so he wouldn't see.

Not that he was looking. For all she knew, he'd fallen back asleep again. A quick glance at the oven said she had forty-five minutes still before the lasagna would come out. She dropped the knife, grabbed her phone, and went right out the back door.

The air in the backyard was stifling. Suffocating. So dang hot. She sucked at it anyway, so many truths crashing into her at the same time.

She'd waited too long.

Been too prideful.

Sacrificed what really mattered most.

She collapsed into a heap on the back steps and cried,

her phone gripped in her hand. She knew who she wanted to call. Knew the number.

Didn't know how it would go.

She dialed her mother anyway.

The phone rang and rang, and just when Sissy was sure it would go to voicemail, her mom said, "Sissy?" with way too much shock in her voice.

"Hey, Mom," she said, looking out over her green lawn. She knew it wouldn't stay that way for long, that summer's hot hand would take the roots and crush them.

"What's going on? Are you okay?"

No, she wasn't. "Yeah, I'm fine," she said. "How are you? I'm thinking I might want to come visit." The loan had gone through and the audit was completed. Last Chance Ranch had a lot of moving parts, sure. From animal adoptions to llama wool being sold, Sissy tracked every penny and every nickel.

But they could do without her for a few days. Or a week. She could fill in spreadsheets and generate reports when she got back.

"Jessie's coming for the Fourth," her mom said.

"I want it to just be us," Sissy said. "Though I might come for the Fourth too, if that's all right." Or if this first visit went okay.

"You don't sound fine," her mom said, and Sissy's first reaction was to ask her how she would even know. They hadn't spoken in so long.

All at once, she realized how she felt about her mother was exactly how Dave felt about her.

Her heart wailed, and her first instinct was to run the way she had the first time she and Dave had broken up. Buy an airplane ticket. Pack a bag. Put all her troubles in the rear-view mirror and pray they'd be gone before she returned.

She squared her shoulders and braced herself. She would not be running again.

"I'm seeing someone," Sissy said. "And I just want to talk to you about him."

"I'm on the night shift until Thursday," she said. "I have Friday and Sunday off, but I have to go in to the hospital on Saturday."

"I'll be there Thursday morning," she said, her pulse doing a little jig at the thought of seeing and speaking to her mother after so long. "Thanks, Mom."

"Bye, sweetie."

The call ended, and Sissy gripped the phone in her fingers until they hurt. Everything hurt right now, and it seemed strange that it wasn't even her own pain that had spurred it.

She heard something in the house behind her, and it could've been her cat. Or it could've been Dave, realizing he'd fallen asleep and that she'd fled the premises.

Employing her rapid texting techniques, she got her fingers moving and started rallying the troops by texting Clara, Kirsten, and Hailey.

Girls night needed. 911. Tomorrow night. My place. Involves my mother.

"What are you doing out here?" Dave asked, and Sissy spun back to him as her friends started responding.

"Just thinking," she said.

"I fell asleep in there," he said. "In like, two seconds."

"I know, cowboy." She tried to smile at him, but her emotions still felt like they'd been encased in gelatin. "Listen, I have some news."

"Intriguing." He yawned, and she wished she'd just ordered pizza. Then they could eat, and he could get on home to bed.

"I'm going to see my mother."

That got him to look at her, curiosity dancing in his eyes. "Oh?"

"Thursday," she said. "I'll be gone for the weekend."

"I'm not coming, I gather."

She shook her head, wondering what *that* reunion would be like. "Not this time."

"What made you decide that?" he asked.

She didn't know what to say, how to explain to him that she hadn't spoken to her mom much over the years since they'd broken up. Or how to explain the knotted feelings inside her. She'd thought she was ready for the next stage of her life: marriage and family.

Now she was realizing she had no idea how she'd deal with her life if she couldn't have those things. And it was a very real possibility that she couldn't.

So why perpetuate a relationship with Dave at all?

She hated that the question existed in her mind, and disliked even more that she didn't have an answer for it.

"You must've felt like you need to go," he finally said. "Is that it?"

"Yeah," she said, seizing onto that very rational reason. "That's it. I have some things I need to talk to her about."

If Sissy could get all the darkness cleared out of her life, maybe she'd know which way to go. Armed with that plan, she went back inside with Dave where it was cool. They chatted and ate, and he never had to know she'd panicked about not having babies of her own.

THE FOLLOWING EVENING, Kirsten arrived first carrying a vat of homemade guacamole and three bags of chips.

Sissy didn't even exclaim that it was too many chips for four of them. She hadn't eaten all day, and she was ready for this binge and spill session. The slow cooker behind her had queso dip in it, and while the cheese wasn't technically organic, and she couldn't pronounce any of the ingredients, she didn't care.

It tasted good with chips, and she plucked one bag from Kirsten's fingers as her friend walked past.

"Your mother?" Kirsten asked, because it was a rule they couldn't ask questions on a 911 text. Just say yes or no if they could come and maybe express some sympathy.

"I haven't seen you in forever," she said. "I feel like I missed something."

"Me too," Sissy said. "And I've been around."

Kirsten gave her a stern glare but continued into the kitchen. "Not Scooter's."

"Well, I don't need Scooter's now that I'm dating Dave."

"So this isn't about Dave?"

Before Sissy could answer, the doorbell rang again, and the door opened without her touching it. Clara and Hailey came bustling in, Hailey with oven mitts on as she carried a cake pan that didn't hold cake.

The salty, creamy, spicy scent that met Sissy's nose meant it was her hot chicken chile dip—also perfect for chips. Clara carried two more bags, as well as a huge glass measuring bowl of homemade salsa.

She handed it to Sissy with the words, "From my mother, who keeps asking me when I'm going to find a nice cowboy like you have. Anyone up at that ranch single?"

Sissy thought through the men at Last Chance Ranch. There were plenty of single men up there, and she said, "Definitely."

"I'd like an invite to something," Clara said with arched eyebrows as she sat at the bar. "You guys didn't start without us, did you?"

"Nope," Kirsten said. "I had just asked her if this was really about Dave and not her mother when you came in."

All three women looked at Sissy for the answer. "Guys, it's not about Dave. If it were, I would've said that." She ripped open a bag of chips and eyed her friends. "What? You think I'd lure you here under false pretenses?" She glanced at the guac. "Maybe for that."

They all laughed, and Sissy sobered first. "No, I had a crash and burn moment last night, and I ended up calling my mom. I'm going to visit her on Thursday." She dipped a chip in the guacamole, the scent of avocado and lemon hitting her nose and making her mouth water.

"I haven't seen her in a decade." Sissy put the chip in her mouth while her friends stared.

"You've never said that," Kirsten said at the same time Clara said, "I can't go ten minutes without talking to my mom."

"Guys," Hailey said. "Let's think about this while we load up our plates. Then I'm sure we'll have some really great advice for Sissy." She nodded like that was that, and sure enough, they all grabbed plates and started piling on the various dips.

Sissy could only hope and pray that they'd have something she could use to get through the visit.

Scratch that. She didn't want to hope for things she had no control over.

So she just prayed.

Chapter Fourteen

Dave's nerves assaulted him all day on Thursday, because he knew Sissy wouldn't be in her office. She wasn't on the ranch at all, and it felt...different without her there. She'd texted him a picture of the beach a couple of hours ago, claiming she'd already made it to San Diego.

He wasn't sure if that was true, because she'd have had to miss all the traffic between the ranch and the beach, and she had to go through LA. So missing traffic was impossible.

Maybe she'd left earlier than he'd thought. He didn't know. What he did know was that something had changed a couple of nights ago while he dozed on her couch. When he'd awakened, she'd been gone, all the vegetables for the salad still sitting on the counter.

She'd covered her distress nicely, and Dave didn't like

that either. He tried not to think about it too much. After all, Sissy was extraordinarily gifted at saying what was on her mind, and she'd never really held back with him before.

A text from Karla came in that said, *Lunch at the homestead, noon – 2. Come whenever.*

His stomach growled, though it was barely ten-thirty.

"Yes," Cache said as if he'd just scored the game-winning touchdown in the Super Bowl. "Lunch at the homestead," he called throughout the barn as if every cowboy there didn't also get the same message from Karla.

He met Dave's eye, that goofy smile on his face, and then ducked his head a moment later. Oh, he definitely had something going on with Karla, but Dave had never brought it up at band practice again.

Their set at Finer Diner had gone well, and Cache had been bent on getting them more gigs. Why he cared, Dave wasn't sure. He knew he wasn't going to be a famous country music star.

"Hey," he said to the other cowboy. "You're still okay to take my chores this weekend? It's the first weekend of the month."

"A-okay," Cache said. "And we're doing practice tonight, right?"

"That's right," Dave said. "Did you hear on that city picnic?"

"They were booked," Cache said, measuring out the exact right bit of medicine he needed for one of the horses.

"Too bad," Dave said, but he didn't really think so. "I'll let Scarlett know you're doing my stuff. You get a bonus."

"I'm aware," Cache said, glancing up. His whole demeanor changed, and Dave saw something there he hadn't seen before. He had no idea what it was, but Cache added, "Thanks for asking me first, Dave."

"Sure thing," he said, peering closer to Cache. "Everything okay?"

"Yep." He went back to the medicines he needed to get out before lunch. "Can you believe Gina's letting me do the meds?"

"She trusts you," Dave said. "She can't be everywhere at once." He felt bad for the large animal care vet, as Gina had dozens and dozens of horses, llamas, pigs, and more to deal with. Some with very specific medical needs. "And I heard she's doing a surgery on a horse down in the valley today."

"Yeah," Cache said. "I shoulda been a vet, bro. They make so much money."

"Do they?" Dave honestly didn't know. "You should go back to school."

Cache scoffed. "Right. I'm too old for that, and I have no money." He tossed Dave a look that said so much, Dave couldn't decipher it all. Cache turned in the next moment, his tray of cocktails ready to go out to the horses who needed them.

Dave watched him go, sure something new was going on inside Cache's mind. He'd worked with the man for almost two years, and he'd never detected any hesitancy in him to do exactly what he wanted. He was an excellent cowboy, quick to laugh, and super opinionated. But one of Dave's best friends.

"Dave," Hudson called from the gaping mouth of the barn. "I need you out here. Fences down and pigs everywhere."

Dave took off at a jog, grabbing a couple of ropes from the pegs by the door just in case Hudson didn't have one yet. He'd worked with the pigs a lot, and while some people might think they couldn't move because of their size, those people would be wrong.

All animals seemed to have a sixth sense about breaks in the fence line too, and he counted no less than six of the porkers had already escaped. Cache stood on the wrong side of the fence, his tray of horse medications balanced in one hand while keeping his eye on the animals in the pen where he was.

"Dave," he said. "Come get this." He lifted the tray over the top rung of the fence, and Dave tossed a rope over the fence as he approached. He grabbed the tray, and as quickly as he could, took it back inside the barn.

When he returned to the scene outside, a couple of pigs had already been corralled back into their field.

He couldn't help laughing at Ames as he dashed after a black and white potbellied pig named Petunia. The mama pig squealed as her stubby legs got her moving faster than the cowboy.

Dave whipped the rope out, hoping he still remembered how to use it. Sure, the animals got out from time to time, but he wasn't the best with a rope. Volunteers appeared on the edge of the fields, and they'd just stand there, making a human fence the pigs wouldn't veer toward.

Just more witnesses to his terrible throwing. But Dave plowed forward anyway, because he had a rope and Ames didn't. How the guy thought he'd catch Petunia, Dave didn't know. But he missed when he threw the rope, so he wasn't much help either.

Hudson roped another one, and Cache whooped as he did too. Dave focused on the pig standing there, her eyes definitely on him. "Come on, girl," he said to the pig—whom he'd bathed in the recent past. "We're friends, right? You've got to go back in the field. It's nice and muddy, just how you like it."

She grunted, and Dave let the rope fly. Gratitude and relief filled him when the rope landed around her neck, and he pulled it tight. Petunia didn't seem to care about the rope, and she started trotting again.

There was no way he could hold back her weight, so he let go of the rope before it burned his hands. Foolishness hit him, but at least there was a lead on her now. A cowboy with gloves could grab it and lean into the pig's flight.

Sure enough, Gray grabbed the rope and dug his feet in. Petunia stilled with the rope cut into her, and Gray got her back in the right spot. Dave hadn't spent much time or attention on the cowboy he'd first taken on a tour of the ranch.

He hadn't had to. He had friends and Sissy, and he was too old to spend time with people he didn't care about. But now, he tipped his hat at the cowboy, who tipped his hat right back.

Sawyer and Carson had lumber out, and they worked on getting the fence back in place.

Life on the ranch went on, the way it always did. Dave would be on his way back to Fort Ivins tomorrow evening, and when he got back on Monday, Sissy would be back.

In the afternoon, he decided he could skip cleaning out the feed bins for the llamas, and he saddled Chestnut and told Hudson he'd be back before dinner. He thought about the way Cache had flirted with Karla during lunch, and how happy Carson and Adele and Sawyer and Jeri were.

Even Hudson and Scarlett, though they were going through something hard, were happy. They loved each other.

All at once, as if the hot sun overhead and the steady clomping of Chestnut's hooves had laid it all out for him, Dave realized something.

Sissy didn't love him—at least not the way the other women loved their men.

"It's still early," he told himself, told the horse. "Right, Chestnut?" He patted the equine's neck, but his curiosity over her sudden visit to her mother raged through him as fast as rapids.

Had she gone there to get advice about how to break up with him a second time?

Feeling like he'd been removed from his own body, he reached for the water bottle in his saddlebag. It was cool, but he could barely get himself to swallow it. What would he do if she ended things again?

He'd never really let himself drift down that road before, but he did now. He thought of Carson, who'd left very soon after Dave had arrived at the ranch. He'd left, because Adele had broken his heart.

Sure, they were both back now, but Dave knew better than most what a long road that was. Heck, he was currently on it.

Should he turn around now, while he still had his dignity?

Chestnut had no answers. Dave had no answers. Even God Himself was silent on the matter.

When Dave arrived at the cabin, he put the horse to pasture and pulled out his phone. He needed to know why Sissy had run to Southern California to see her mother.

"Hey, there," she said after she answered, her voice full of playfulness. "What are you doing this afternoon?"

"I came out to the cabin," he said.

"You did? Aren't you going to the base tomorrow?"

"Yeah, and I have band practice tonight."

"So you're just skipping out on chores." She laughed,

and Dave sure did like the sound of it. Such a reaction from her almost always soothed him, brought him a measure of happiness. But today, his stomach was still angry and didn't want to be soothed.

"A little bit," he said. "Sissy, I have a question for you."

"Sure," she said, clearly not concerned.

"Why did you go to San Diego to see your mom?" Dave gazed up into the sky, the blueness of it almost too perfect.

She sighed, and Dave got at least part of the answer he wanted. "Do you really want to know?"

"Of course I do," he said. "Have I given you the impression I don't want to know about your life?"

"No, of course not."

"Something happened the other night," he said. "I don't know what it was, and it's fine if you need some time to work through it."

"I do, a little," she said.

"So you'll tell me when you're ready." Dave could live with that. He could.

"I can tell you some now," she said, but then she remained quiet.

Dave didn't want to beg her. Frustration mingled with his curiosity, making a dangerous cocktail in his gut.

And still Sissy didn't speak.

"It's fine—" he started just as she said, "I haven't spoken to my mom in a long, long time."

Chapter Fifteen

S issy pressed her eyes closed. She'd probably started in the wrong spot.

"What?" Dave asked. "You guys have always been close."

"No," Sissy said slowly. "That was the old me. The me from almost twenty years ago." She sighed and turned away from the sight of her mother at a table down the sidewalk a little bit. When she'd seen Dave's name on the screen, Sissy had said, "This is him, Mom," and excused herself.

"The truth is, when I broke up with you, my mother was very angry."

"She was?" Dave sounded all kinds of surprised.

"She adored you," Sissy said. "And she thought I was foolish for breaking up with you so I could travel." Just saying the words made Sissy feel like she'd done something wrong all over again.

But it had been *her* life. *Her* decision to make. And she had wanted to do all the things she'd done.

"And yes," she said when Dave remained silent. "Something happened the other night. You told me Scarlett couldn't have kids, and I panicked. I needed someone to talk to, and I ended up calling my mother and setting up this weekend visit."

"I told you that?"

"Yes," Sissy said. "You were half-asleep, I think."

"I don't think that's common knowledge, Sissy," he said. "I didn't know I'd told you."

"I haven't said anything to anyone," she said. "And I won't."

"Thank you."

"Anyway." She blew out her breath. "I wanted to talk to my mom about you. About not being able to have kids." Her throat closed so unexpectedly, her emotions shooting into her sinuses and burning the backs of her eyes.

"You can't have children either?"

"I'm old, Dave," she said, her voice too high and so nasally. "I missed my chance. We missed our chance." Her voice broke, and the tears she never wanted to show appeared. She swallowed, trying to get control. "I screwed up. I chose hiking in the Alps over having babies with you."

"Sissy," he said, not unkindly. But he didn't say she

was wrong. Didn't say they still had time. She wasn't wrong, and they didn't have any more time.

"I'm just waiting for you to break up with me," she said honestly, swiping at her face as her mom looked over her shoulder to see where Sissy had gotten to.

"Why would I do that?"

"Because Dave, you deserve someone who puts marriage and family first. That's not me." She gave a bitter laugh, wishing she could rewind time and keep all the knowledge she had now.

"Sissy, there are so many ways to be a mother."

"I don't want to hear them," she said. "Not right now."

"Okay." He gave off the sense of defeat in his voice. "And Sissy, I know this is going to scare you, and I don't want to do that. Maybe I'll just save it for when I can see you again."

"If you're going to break up with me, maybe you should just do it," she said.

He sighed, and she didn't like the heaviness in it. She hated that they were having this conversation on the phone instead of in person. She wanted to see his face, watch his body language, kiss him afterward.

"Sissy, I know you're not a stupid woman. But you're being really stupid about this."

Instant anger flared through her. "About what?"

"About me."

"What about you?"

"There has only ever been one person for me, Sissy,

and that's you." He didn't stutter, and he didn't skip any syllables. The words were just laid out there for her to hear.

"I told you it would scare you," he said.

"You deserve better than me." Someone younger, with more time to reproduce. Someone who could cook, and liked to...make applesauce from scratch. Or something. Sissy wasn't sure exactly what domesticated women did.

"Look," he said, and she could tell the conversation was about to end. "If you're going to break up with me again, can you please do it while I'm at the base this weekend? Then I can find another ranch and another job, and just—I don't know. Start my life again." He was frustrated and angry, and Sissy knew how he felt.

What she didn't know was how she'd gone from flirty and playful and looking forward to answering his call, to this. They'd maybe been on the phone for ten minutes. Maybe.

"I'm not going to break up with you this weekend," she said.

"All right," he said, obviously still a bit dubious. "So I'll see you on Monday?"

"Monday," she confirmed. They said their good-byes, and Sissy drew in a deep breath as she walked back over to the table where her mother sat.

"Everything okay?" she asked.

"Fine." Sissy put a smile on her face. "Did you see who was calling?"

"No, you snatched the phone up like it might explode if you didn't answer immediately." Her mom smiled at her, and Sissy could admit that her mom had been wonderful and gracious and kind about Sissy's reappearance in Southern California.

"It was Dave Merrill," she said, reaching for her iced tea. "You remember him, don't you?"

Her mom blinked, her mouth hanging open. "David Merrill? The man you were supposed to marry?"

"The one you loved," Sissy said with a grin. "The one you told me I'd regret forever if I broke up with him."

"Well, I can't—how did you reconnect?"

"He works at the ranch."

Her mother looked absolutely delighted. "What a coincidence."

"Quite," Sissy said. At least Dave's call had made it easy to tell her mom who she was dating. She'd arrived in town early, being unable to sleep the night before. She'd spent the morning at the beach, because the waves and sunshine soothed her, and she needed a few hours to herself. Just her and her thoughts.

She'd met her mom at the house, and they'd had lunch before they'd decided to do a little shopping.

"How's Jess?"

"Oh, we're not to Jess," her mom said. "Tell me more about Dave."

"What about him? He's about the same. Older. A little grayer." She smiled. "But almost the same."

Almost was the key word, because Dave wasn't exactly the same. He had some issues to work through. He wasn't perfect, and he didn't forgive easily. Everything she'd said to him on the phone streamed through her, and she felt it all keenly.

She wasn't sure why he was so interested in her. She had nothing to offer him, and he was smart enough to know it.

"Did he ever get married?"

"No," Sissy said.

"So no children."

"No children." Sissy played with her napkin, relieved when the waitress returned and asked if they were ready to order.

"Just the tea for me," her mom said.

"I'll take the chocolate cake," Sissy said. No, she didn't need the extra calories. But she sure did need the sugar.

Her mother sipped her iced tea and stirred the straw around, making the ice clink into the glass. She watched Sissy like she had something to say, but she remained silent.

"Mom, I'm afraid I've waited too long to get married." The words just blurted out of Sissy's mouth. Whatever her mother had been planning to say stayed dormant.

Her eyes widened again, a slip of surprise moving through them. Then she reached over and put her hand over Sissy's. "Maybe," she said, and that was all.

Sissy almost preferred a lecture. Some way she could

rage and get all of her feelings out. An argument where she could defend her life choices and feel good about herself again.

The chocolate cake came, and the waitress had brought two forks. Sissy pushed one toward her mom and said, "Don't make me eat this by myself."

Her mother picked up the fork and took a bite of the chocolate cake. It was sweet and rich and heavenly in Sissy's mouth.

"Sissy," her mom said. "You can't change what's happened. Trust me when I say I spent so many years trying to do that."

"Yeah?" Sissy asked.

"When your father left, I wanted to go back and see if I could've made him stay. If I would've just done this, or done that." She shook her head. "The reality is, you have no way of knowing. You and Dave could've gotten married when you were twenty-five, and your life wouldn't have been what you wanted. Or it might have been. You might have had ten babies, or none at all. You might have moved all over the word or stayed right here. You just don't know."

Sissy could hear the wisdom in her words. See the pain on her face when she talked about Sissy's dad. "I know."

"So what's the real problem? If you want to marry Dave, is he not willing?"

"I think he probably is," Sissy said, his words ringing in

her ears. "He wants to be a father." She shrugged and dug into the cake again. "I'm forty-three years old."

"Ah." Her mom nodded and scooped up another bite of cake. "So you didn't wait too long to get married." She looked at Sissy, the same dark eyes shining out of her mother's face that she possessed. "You're worried you waited too long to have a family."

"Yeah," Sissy said. "That about sums it up."

"And that's why you called me earlier this week."

"Yes." Sissy ducked her head, though she wasn't sure why. "I was just missing you, and I wanted to talk to someone about it."

"You haven't said anything to Dave?"

"I have," she said. "He says there's lots of ways to get a baby."

"He's right."

"I know," Sissy said, sighing and looking away. How could she explain how she felt? "I just kind of want my own kids."

"They will be yours," her mom said. "The heart has an unlimited capacity to love."

Sissy heard all the love in her mother's voice, and it drew her back to her. "I'm sorry I ran away all those years ago."

Her mom waved one hand. "Honey, you were on your own path. You loved it, and while I didn't agree with it, you never did anything to me you need to apologize for."

Slowly, the rest of the cake got eaten, and finally, her mom said, "I started seeing someone a few months ago."

Sissy's eyes widened as a smile spread across her face. "Mom. You did?"

"Don't look at me like that."

"Like what?" Sissy said, scraping her fork across the plate though she'd already gotten all the chocolate she could.

"Like I haven't dated, ever."

Sissy giggled, covering her mouth with one hand. Her mother smiled too, and Sissy let her laughter fly. "Mom, you haven't dated in *for*ever. Who is this guy?"

"I met him at the bookshop."

"Ooh, the bookshop," Sissy said, adopting an English accent. Some of her worries and cares over her possible infertility and her definite inferiority complex with Dave disappeared, and she enjoyed her afternoon and evening with her mother.

DAVE NEVER STRAYED TOO FAR from her mind, even though the weekend was fun. More fun than Sissy had had with her family in a long, long time. She met her mom's boyfriend, and he clearly adored her. Adam was older, like her mom, and he had four children.

Her mother's comment about having a heart that could love limitlessly suddenly made more sense, and

Sissy was so glad she'd followed the prompting to call her mother when she was distressed the other night.

As she drove north on Sunday night, she put the window down and just enjoyed herself. Dave wouldn't be at the ranch when she went in tomorrow, and she was actually glad. Now that she'd confessed that she felt inadequate to be with him, they could start to work through things.

She hoped.

She knew that she would not be the one to break up with him. Not this time. If their relationship was going to end, he was going to have to do it. Sissy almost texted her friends when she pulled into her driveway that evening, but she decided she needed to figure out how to be alone.

For someone who'd done so much by herself, she sure didn't like spending time with her thoughts. Tonight, she went into her backyard and sat on the steps where she'd been when she'd called her mother.

Letting her thoughts go wherever they wanted, she gazed around, thinking she'd like a dog to spend her evenings with. Of course, she'd been busy with Dave in the evenings, and he had a canine already.

So no dog.

"You don't need a dog," she told herself, her voice loud among the whispering breeze in her backyard.

She definitely felt like she needed something, but she wasn't sure *what*.

"What should I do?" she asked the sky. The wind

picked up, almost like God was trying to say something back to her. The words got whipped away before she could truly hear what they were saying.

"I don't want to leave Last Chance Ranch," she said, and she knew that. She liked her job there. Loved it, in fact. She liked the people there. Scarlett, and Adele, and all of the other women. She loved the goat yoga. She was very good at her job.

"So am I doing what I'm meant to do with my life?" she wondered. A sense of peace came over her, and she told herself to stop worrying so much. She had a good job. A gorgeous boyfriend. Fun friends. She'd been all over the world, seen and done things not many people had the opportunity to do.

She couldn't have everything, could she? Was she a bad person if she wanted it all? Wanted the house, the white picket fence, the job, the man, the kids—on top of the amazing life she'd already had?

Sissy couldn't think about it anymore, and she went inside to go to bed so she could just *stop thinking*.

That certainly didn't work, but she managed to get some sleep and get to work on time the next morning. Since she'd been gone for a couple of days, she had plenty to do to distract her—thankfully.

Dave didn't usually get back until mid-afternoon from his military weekends, and as the clock ticked closer and closer to that time, her heart began to dance around inside her chest. Would he come see her right away? Check in with Cache, who usually took over his chores for him? Was he as anxious to see her as she was to see him?

What would she even say to him when he finally walked in?

She pushed all the questions—so many blasted questions—out of her mind and focused on the numbers. Numbers didn't lie. Numbers always added up, and they didn't leave her wondering why something hadn't worked out.

Five o'clock came, and she hadn't seen Dave yet. Anxiety blipped through her with every heartbeat as she shut down her computer and got ready to go home.

But she wasn't going to go home. She was going to find Dave and they were going to work things out. Her decision made, she pulled out her phone and texted him.

Where are you? Did you make it back to the ranch okay?

Home, his response came almost immediately.

Can I stop by?

Of course.

Sissy wished she'd had more than coffee on the way to the ranch to put in her stomach, but she hadn't packed a lunch. By the time she went up the steps at Dave's cabin, her stomach was positively shaking.

He opened the door before she knocked, and he looked casual and comfortable in a pair of gym shorts and a T-shirt that said GO ARMY across the front of it. He still wore the cowboy hat, of course, but nothing on his feet, and he looked delicious and exhausted at the same time.

"Hey," he said, a smile touching his lips.

"Hey." She moved right into his arms, and it was easy. "I missed you."

"Yeah?"

"Yeah."

He held her, and they swayed for a few minutes. Then he finally said, "Come in, and let's talk."

Chapter Sixteen

Dave had endured a rough weekend, but Sissy had come to him, and he wasn't going to turn her away. "Are you hungry?" he asked, closing the door behind her.

"Yeah," she said. "I didn't bring lunch today."

"Why not?"

"Just forgot," she said, removing her heels and leaving them by his front door.

Dave wasn't sure he believed her, but he didn't want to push her on it. He'd been wrestling with her image of him for days, and he was simply too tired. He was *not* perfect, and he couldn't deal with the weight of it.

He took her hand and played with her fingers. "How was your visit with your mom?"

"Great," she said, and when he looked into her eyes, he could tell she meant it. "We talked about a lot, and it was just exactly what I needed."

"I'm glad," he said.

She put both hands on his chest, sending pops of attraction through him. He couldn't believe he'd told her she was the only woman for him. He might as well have opened up his chest and told her to start sawing his heart out.

She tipped up onto her toes and kissed him, and Dave sure liked the sweet taste of her mouth. She was minty, and it made his lips tingle. "I'm sorry I freaked out last week," she whispered.

"Is that what that was?" he asked, touching his lips to her chin and then her neck.

"Yeah, I just...think too much."

"So that hasn't changed about you." He chuckled and pulled away, starting to feel himself slipping in his resolve to keep things between them on safe ground. He found everything about her desirable, and surely she knew that.

"Some things die hard." She grinned at him. "Rough weekend?"

"Yes," he said simply, not wanting to get into it. "I stopped on my way home and grabbed a pizza."

"Ah, anticipating me coming over?" She followed him into the kitchen, and gladness spread through Dave as she did.

"Hoping," he said. And yet, he hadn't texted her. Hadn't invited her. It felt nice to have her come to him, when he felt like he'd been pursuing her for so long. No, he hadn't gone to China, or Switzerland, or Chile, but he still felt like he'd been following her all over the world, patiently waiting for her to come back to him.

He opened the fridge and took the take-and-bake pizza out. It would be ready in a half an hour, and if they talked much longer than that, Dave might lose his mind. He started preheating the oven and unwrapping the pizza.

"I just have to say one thing," he said. "About last week. Is that okay?"

"Yes," she said.

He looked at her, feeling dangerous and unsettled. "I'm not perfect, and I think it's really dangerous of you to think I am."

"I never said you were perfect."

"You implied it," he said. "By saying I deserve someone better than you. Sissy, there *is* no one better than you."

"Dave—"

"I don't mean that in a romantic way," he said, realizing what he'd said a moment too late. "I mean, you're kind. You're thoughtful. You're smart. You're professional. You have faith, and you care about people. You're a *great* person." He knew he was coming across a little too intense, but he couldn't help himself.

"I know you're not perfect," she said after a pause. "After all, you're being really bossy right now."

"Bossy?" He shook his head, but he couldn't help smiling. "I'm not being bossy. I'm being *nice*."

Sissy got up from where she'd sat at the dining room table and approached him. "You *are* nice."

"So are you."

"So we're equally nice." Sissy reached up and removed his hat, leaving Dave feeling a little too exposed. "And silver. And sexy. And I'm sorry I added to your stress this weekend."

"You didn't," he said, thinking of their insane training this weekend. "I was too tired to think much about it."

"Yeah, right," she said with a smile. "You think as much as I do."

Dave smiled down at her. "Maybe you're right."

"Oh, I'm right, Mister Merrill." She laughed, and Dave joined her, glad their talk didn't need to be too terribly long tonight. He liked it when she called him Mister Merrill—something she'd done when they were twenty-somethings falling in love.

"Anything you need to say to me before we just crash on the couch?"

He watched a perfect storm of things roll across her face. "I've had a good life, and I think you were right when you said there are a lot of ways to get a baby."

Dave kissed her, letting himself go a little too far for just a moment. "If you want a baby, sweetheart, I'll marry you tomorrow and do everything I can to make it happen."

Sissy froze, and Dave's suspicions that she wasn't as ready as she thought she was gelled. "You would?"

"Absolutely." He kissed her throat, really enjoying the

way she tipped her head back for him. "And I'd really like the baby-making part that came after the wedding."

"Dave," she said, a hint of embarrassment in her voice. She pulled away from him, and her face was bright red.

"Ah, you haven't thought that far ahead, have you?" He kept the grin on his face, realizing the difference between men and women very keenly in that moment.

"Maybe," she said, turning her back on him. "I don't think...anyone would want to do that with me."

"Really?" Dave snaked his arms around her. "Why not? You're gorgeous. You're sexy. You smell great." He took a deep breath of her hair, growling a little to add some playfulness to this serious conversation.

"Is that all it takes? Some orange-scented shampoo?" She laughed, and Dave joined her. "And I don't smell great. It's hot in the admin building, and I've been sweating all day."

"You smell great to me," he said, releasing her when she wiggled away from him. He wasn't sure if he was being rejected or not, so he turned back to the oven only to see the pizza wasn't close to coming out yet.

"I don't feel gorgeous or sexy," she said.

He looked at her as he settled his cowboy hat back on his head. "How can I help you with that? Because you're both. All the time."

"All the time? Even when I get out of bed?"

"Especially when you get out of bed. I mean." He rubbed his hand up the back of his neck, the hair there suddenly too long and pulling in his hat band. "In my imagination. I've never woken up next to you."

"Your imagination?" Her eyebrows went up. "Do you *fantasize* about me, Mister Merrill?"

"Come on," he said, turning away. Of course he did. But he said, "I'm not a pervert."

"I don't think you are." She came up beside him. "I think about us, married," she said. "But I don't want you to marry me tomorrow and try to give me what you think I want."

"You don't want a baby?"

"I do, but I think there's a time and place for everything, and I don't think either of us are ready for marriage."

Dave wasn't sure what vibe he was giving off, but he could definitely feel an unready vibe from Sissy. Which was fine. It wasn't his biological clock ticking.

"I just want you to be happy," he said.

"I am," she said.

"Good." The timer on the oven went off, and Dave had never felt more saved by a bell than he did in that moment. "Then let's eat, and then you can curl into me while I sleep on the couch. Deal?"

The best word on the planet was, "Deal," spoken in Sissy's voice.

A WEEK PASSED, and then two. Friday night found Dave packing his guitar beside him in the truck, with Sissy over by the window. No band practice tonight, but a gig in Lancaster. Sawyer was bringing Jeri and Brayden. Lance had his new girlfriend in the truck behind him, and Cache had steadfastly refused to invite someone. Dave wasn't sure why he didn't just ask Karla, as it was obvious the two of them had a thing going.

Dave wasn't all that in to hiding how he felt about someone, and he and Sissy had been doing just fine since their tense weekend a couple of weeks ago.

"Are you nervous?" she asked him.

"No," he said.

"Not even a little?"

He glanced at her. "Why should I be? It's just playing the guitar and singing."

"In front of people."

"I know we're not pros," he said. "But we put on a good show. I know that too." He didn't mean to sound arrogant. Was stating facts arrogance? "Cache wants to take us farther," Dave said. "But I don't get why. We're busy here at the ranch, and it's not like we're going to tour."

"That Cache is an exuberant guy," Sissy said, which made Dave laugh.

"That he is." Dave rolled down his window and let the summer evening air in as he turned up the radio. He started singing along, and Sissy giggled at his over-the-top theatrics.

"You have a great voice," she said.

"Have you not heard me sing in the band?" Dave turned down the radio as he looked at her, sure she'd seen him. Hadn't she?

"No," she said. "That night you were at Finer Diner, I had girl's night, remember?"

"Yeah," he said. "You're right. I guess I just didn't realize." He grinned at her. "We're good. I mean, Last Chance Cowboys are *good*."

"That's why you're playing at a rodeo in Lancaster?" She cocked her right eyebrow at him.

"Yes," he said. "Rodeos are a good time, Sissy. Have you ever been?"

"To a rodeo?"

"Yes, ma'am," he said. "To a rodeo." She'd been all over the world, and she hadn't been to a rodeo?

"Well, not recently."

"Not ever," he said, chuckling.

"So why are we driving to Lancaster for a rodeo when there's one in Pasadena?" She shook her phone at him as if she'd just looked up what a rodeo was.

"Because Cache booked us at this one," Dave said. "And it's good money. A few hundred dollars each."

"All right," she said. "It's just a long way for a few hundred dollars."

"It's an hour," he said. "Just relax and enjoy the ride."

He turned the radio back up and sang along with every song he knew.

He met up with the other guys, and Cache was definitely the most keyed up. They checked in with the master of ceremonies, strapped on their instruments, and Lance made sure his drums were set up on the platform next to the area where the MC stood.

"Ready?" Cache asked, glancing around and still fiddling with his hat and then his strap.

"Yes," Sawyer said, his eyes out in the crowd. Sissy sat next to Jeri, and she had the baby on her lap. Dave sure liked the sight of that, and he hoped that if he and Sissy did get married, she'd open her mind to adoption.

Lance's girlfriend, Kaylee, sat next to them, and she was a fun woman with a lot of blonde hair. A bit young in Dave's opinion, but Dave didn't have to date her.

"So what's with you and Karla?" Dave asked, and Cache almost fell down.

"What?"

"Oh, come on," Dave said. "Everyone knows you like her."

Cache looked around, and even Sawyer had been drawn into this conversation. "He's right," Sawyer said.

"Lance?"

"Totally obvious."

Cache turned a shade of red Dave hadn't seen in a while. "There's nothing with me and Karla," he said.

"Let's just play." He stomped over to the platform and stood behind his mic.

Dave chuckled, only feeling a bit bad for calling him out. He got behind the mic in the front and turned to the rest of the guys. "We ready?"

"So ready," Lance said.

Before anyone else could answer, the MC practically screamed into the mic, "And now, all the way from a rescue ranch near Pasadena, we've got the Last—Chance—Cowbooooooooys!"

Cache yelled, "One, two, one, two, three, four," and everyone started to play.

Dave spun back to the microphone, pure adrenaline flowing through him. He could admit he loved the rush of performing, and the sea of faces before him blurred together.

All but one—Sissy's.

She wore a huge smile and danced with that baby, and Dave decided he was all the way in love with her.

Chapter Seventeen

S issy thoroughly enjoyed the rodeo. Kissing Dave after and exclaiming about how good he was. When he dropped her off at her house, she kissed him and said he was *hot* up there on that stage.

She liked eating lunch with him, and she was seriously considering taking him home to her Mom's Fourth of July picnic. With only a week to go, she still hadn't asked him. She wasn't sure why she was nervous about it. Jessie and her mother had met Dave before.

With only a few days to go, and preparations in full swing around the ranch for the big picnic Scarlett and Hudson put on in the backyard of the homestead every year, she decided she had to ask him that day. Otherwise, she'd have to drive to San Diego by herself for the holiday.

But it was an overnight trip, and she wasn't sure if...she wasn't sure what she wasn't sure about. She rolled over in bed and picked up her phone. *Want to go to my mother's for the Fourth?*

She stared at the words in her message, her heart pounding in her chest. She sent it and went to get in the shower so she wouldn't be able to field any questions.

The fact that she was nervous to ask him to a simple picnic plagued her, and she didn't know what was wrong with her. She liked Dave. She *really* liked Dave. They'd talked about marriage and kids, and yet, she felt stuck.

She couldn't move forward with Dave. She couldn't go back. She couldn't break up with him. She couldn't break his heart like that. And yet, he didn't seem to be anxious to move forward either.

"What do you want him to do?" she asked herself as she shaved her legs. "Propose?"

She stilled, wondering what that would look like this time. Last time, there had been candles and roses. A table on the beach. Him down on one knee, with the biggest diamond he could buy at the time. On his Army salary, it wasn't huge, but she'd been so happy.

What would he do this time?

In that moment, Sissy knew one thing—Dave would *not* be asking her to marry him this time. No, if she wanted the house, the white picket fence, the husband, the kids, *she* was going to have to ask *him*.

"No wonder he's done nothing," she said, all kinds of lightbulbs going off in her head. "He's gone as far as he's willing to go. He doesn't want to get his heart broken again."

Of course he didn't. She didn't want to break it again either. But could she really propose to him?

Her phone started ringing from the bedroom, and she hurried through the rest of her shower. She got dressed and dried her hair before she checked her phone. Dave had called, and she tapped, swiped, and tapped again to call him back.

"Hey," she said. "Sorry, in the shower."

"Your mother's for a Fourth picnic?"

"That's a no?"

"It's a I-didn't-know-that-was-happening."

"Well, it is."

"Why didn't you mention it before now?"

"I don't know," Sissy said.

"I told Scarlett I'd help with all the setup."

Sissy blew out her breath. "There are a dozen cowboys here to help set up the tent." She cocked her head, trying to figure out the reason he didn't want to go.

"Yeah," he said.

"You don't want to go," she said.

"Not particularly."

"Why not?"

He cleared his throat. "Can I tell you at lunch?"

"Really?"

"Yeah, I have to run."

"Okay," she said, barely getting the two-syllable word

out before the call ended. Sissy looked at her phone like it had turned into a snake. "What is going on?"

She felt a little sick as she finished getting ready, taking extra care to put on jewelry and just the right amount of lip gloss. By the time her tires went from paved road to gravel as she approached the ranch, her heartbeat was positively tapdancing in her chest.

The robot mailbox that welcomed everyone to Last Chance Ranch waved to her, and since she'd been here last, someone had put red, white, and blue streamers in his hands. Scarlett was always doing something festive with her beloved Prime, and Sissy smiled at the robot as if he could smile back.

On a whim, she turned into the homestead's driveway instead of continuing past the way she normally did. Well, recently, she'd been stopping at Jeri's, but Brayden was sleeping more now, and Sissy had quit going over early in the morning.

The scent of bacon floated on the air, and she really hoped it was coming from inside the homestead. She knocked, almost like she didn't want anyone to know she was there, and she stood back to wait.

Several seconds later, a curious Scarlett opened the door, obviously not expecting a visitor before breakfast. "Sissy," she said with surprise in her voice. Instant concern entered her expression. "What's going on?"

"Nothing. I—" Her throat closed, and she didn't know what to say.

"Come in," she said. "Are you hungry? Hudson's just making eggs right now."

Sissy nodded, though the thought of putting anything in her mouth made her gag. She went into the kitchen, a little nervous to say anything in front of Hudson. Dave seemed to be better friends with Cache, Sawyer, and Lance—his bandmates—but the ranch operated like a small town. Gossip flew, and if she wasn't careful Dave could hear about this conversation before lunchtime. He didn't like to be talked about behind his back, and Sissy realized coming here was a bad idea.

"I'm going to go shower." Hudson placed a kiss on Scarlett's cheek and smiled at Sissy. "Heya, Sissy."

She mustered up a wave before he left, and she sat at the table. Scarlett put a plate in front of her and brought over the bacon and eggs. She sat too, and said, "Talk."

Sissy lifted one shoulder instead, the words damming up behind her vocal cords.

"Okay," Scarlett said, taking a few pieces of bacon. "I'll talk then." She took a deep breath and kept her eyes on her plate. "Seems to me like you and Dave are getting along. A bump here. A bruise there. Normal stuff every couple goes through." She bit off a piece of bacon and chewed it, leaving a gap for silence.

Sissy didn't like it. Had never really liked being alone with her thoughts. She filled her time with adventure, with new places, new friends, new experiences.

"But," Scarlett said, emphasizing the T-sound. "I

suspect you feel like it's going nowhere. I know he feels that way. He's in love with you, but he can't do anything about it."

"What does that mean?" Sissy asked, her voice soft and barely audible to her own ears.

"It means, Sissy, that he's sacrificed all he can. For where he is now, for where you guys have come from, this is all he can give."

This.

What was *this?*

"So what do I do?"

"Well." Scarlett's tone was light, almost a sing-song. "You have lots of choices. But you have to decide if you want Dave in your life or not."

"I do." And Sissy did.

"Then *do something.* You have to *do something.* I don't think it even matters what it is. Just *do something.*" Scarlett scooped some eggs on her plate, and Hudson reappeared in the kitchen, dressed in similar clothes but with damp hair. He settled his cowboy hat on his head and pulled his boots on.

"You're not eating?" Scarlett asked.

"I'll take it with me," he said. "Dave's already out in the field, and he says we have a problem."

"What kind of problem?"

"Something with the pipes." Hudson grabbed a handful of bacon and forked a couple of bites of eggs into his mouth. He swallowed, kissed Scarlett, and added,

"He's already got it fixed, babe. Don't worry. I'll call you later."

"Text me details."

"Yep." And with that, Hudson disappeared out the back door.

Watching them interact was so cute. They were so easy together. So natural. Sissy felt like she was dancing on eggshells in heels, trying not to break anything. She got up, unable to be in the homestead any longer.

"Thanks, Scarlett," Sissy said, heading for the front door.

"You didn't eat either," she called after her.

"I'm not hungry." Sissy paused at the front door. "What do you think I should do?"

Scarlett stood up and approached her. "I don't know, honey." She reached up and tucked Sissy's hair behind her ear. "Either put him out of his misery or marry him."

"Those are my only two choices?" Both made her stomach squirm even more, and she wasn't even sure why. She wanted to run. Get online and find the first flight out of the nearest airport. Get away for a few days. Clear her head. Figure out what she wanted and how to get it.

You want Dave.

"No," Scarlett said. "But he deserves the truth. If you're not willing to marry him, he should know. Then he can make a decision too."

Sissy nodded and left, the short drive over to the Administration Annex passing quickly. She sat behind her desk and fiddled around on her computer for several minutes. Maybe a half-hour. She wasn't sure. Her mind wasn't in a good spot, and while she had work to do, she couldn't focus.

Another quarter was ending tomorrow, and she needed to get reports done. Budgets had already been approved and sent to the various areas of the ranch for the third quarter, and she finally buried her thoughts about Dave beneath numbers and charts, spreadsheets and filing. After all, she could make all of that fall into line nicely, something she couldn't do with her emotions.

Lunchtime came, and Sissy's stomach roared at her for food. Karla had texted that there would be a soup and salad bar in the backyard, and Sissy grew tired of waiting for Dave to show up. Hudson had mentioned that problem out in the fields, and maybe it was bigger than he'd led Scarlett to believe.

No matter what, the window for lunch was ending by the time Sissy sunk her heels into the grass back at the homestead. Male laughter rang out, punching her in the gut.

Dave was here.

"No," Sissy whispered to herself. He'd said he'd come talk to her at lunch. Why hadn't he stopped by the admin building to get her? They could've come over together.

She minced her way along the side of the house, the backyard finally coming into view. Two tables had been set up under the tent attached to the third cabin in the row at the back of the property, as usual. A fan blew, trying to warn off the mid-summer California heat, also as usual.

Men ate at the tables. Normal.

Dave sat with them when he'd said he'd talk to Sissy at lunchtime.

So not normal.

Fire licked its way up her stomach, and she marched toward him, ready to do that something Scarlett had spoken of earlier today. As fast as her fury had roared to life, it faded. She wasn't the type to make a scene, and she didn't want to argue with Dave in front of everyone. Her presence here would be enough for him to see she knew what he'd done. Then they could take their issues behind closed doors.

Her hands shook as she picked up a plate and a bowl. "Hey, Karla," she said loudly. "This looks so good."

"You've got a couple of choices," Karla said from behind the table. "This is sausage tortellini soup. Or the regular chicken noodle." She looked at Sissy for her choice.

"Sausage tortellini." She wasn't sure why anyone would eat soup in the summer, but Karla was an excellent cook, and she ladled soup into Sissy's bowl. She moved down to build her salad, and when she had her food ready, she turned back to the tables.

She'd deliberately kept her back to everyone, trying not to listen. But she wasn't deaf, and she'd heard the silence fall over the tables. A few cowboys had picked up the conversation again, but there was no loud laughter from Dave and his crew.

Three seats remained at his table, and Sissy had never had a problem inserting herself into a crowd. But today, she looked at them for a long moment and moved over to the second table, where Amber sat with Adele, their heads bent together over something Cache was showing them.

"Can I sit with you guys?" she asked brightly, swinging around so her back was to Dave. Actual physical pain dove through her at her snub of him. But hadn't he started it? It was almost two o'clock. When did he think she ate lunch?

Sometimes you don't even stop to eat lunch, she thought, but she pushed it away.

"Yeah, you're just who we need to talk to," Cache said, a bright smile on his face.

"Oh yeah?" Sissy sat down and picked up her spoon. "What about?"

"Cow cuddling," Adele said, and Sissy almost dropped her utensil again.

"I'm sorry. What?"

"You tell her Cache." Adele beamed at the cowboy, and Karla came over and sat beside him too. He glanced at her and then back to Sissy, his face turning a bit red.

He cleared his throat. "I've been working with my

cows," he started. "And Adele trained all the goats for the yoga program."

"Amber trains them now," Adele said.

"Yeah, I know," Cache said. "But you did. And you started this program everyone thought was crazy, but it wasn't. Anyway, there's this thing called cow cuddling. People come out to the ranch, and they get to...spend time with the cattle. I've been teaching them to lay down and let me 'cuddle' into them." He made air quotes around the word cuddle, and Sissy glanced around to see if she was being tricked.

"And people pay for this," she said.

"Yeah," he said.

"They pay a lot," Amber said. She turned her phone toward Sissy.

"Three hundred dollars?" Sissy abandoned her food then to take the phone from Amber. "A new wellness trend." She read, her eyes not able to move fast enough. "Two people. Ninety minutes. Fascinating." She handed the phone back to Amber. "And we want to do this at Last Chance Ranch?"

"Yes," Adele and Cache said at the same time. "It brings in money for the ranch, and people learn about what we do here. We can send them over to volunteer, or to adopt animals, and they get to learn about cattle."

"They brush them down," Cache said. "I teach them a little about the cows. They get to pet them, play with them, and cuddle—if they want."

Sissy had no idea what to say. "And you need money to start? Is that why you need to talk to me?"

"We need an account, yes," Cache said. "We've already got registrations. But we need an account set up for us, and we'll put in a budget, all of that."

Sissy smiled at him, at his nervous energy. She'd never seen Cache anything but confident in his work or laughing with his friends. This new side of him was fun to see. "You have no idea what 'all of that' means, do you?"

"No clue," he said with a grin.

Sissy and the others laughed. She said, "Come over to my office whenever. I'll get you what you need, and we'll go over it."

"Great." He beamed at her, and everyone got up to leave. Lunch was clearly over. No one else had come after her, and she didn't want to be the uncool kid left at the table while everyone else went out to recess.

She hadn't finished, but she could eat at her desk as easily as she could at a table in a sweltering backyard. So she got up too, gathered her utensils, and started back toward her office.

"Can we talk?" Dave asked, falling into step beside her.

She jumped, surprised at his sudden appearance, seemingly out of nowhere. "You scared me."

"Sorry," he said. "I was just waiting for you to finish your conversation."

Sissy looked up at him, trying to figure out what was going on. "You talk."

He obviously didn't like that, because a frown pulled across his features. Sissy cared, but not enough to say anything.

He said he'd come see her at lunch and didn't? He could start the conversation.

Chapter Eighteen

D ave tried to quell the raging storm in his chest, but nothing he did worked. "I don't want to go to San Diego, because I'm not ready to meet your mother."

"You've already met my mother." Sissy could really stride in those heels, even across grass. She possessed some sort of superpower, in Dave's opinion, to be able to walk in shoes like that at all.

She reached the road and paused, looking up at him. "Why don't you just tell me what's really going on?"

"There's nothing going on," he said in a burst. "That's just it, Sissy. There's *nothing* going on."

They'd talked and talked and talked. About kids. About adoption. About waiting too long. About family. About *every*thing.

Dave was done talking.

He wasn't quite sure when he'd reached that decision,

but that was where he'd found himself that morning when she'd oh-so-casually mentioned the picnic at her mother's place—in five days.

Sissy stared at him for a moment longer, and he thought his heart would crack right in half. She had nothing to say either?

She turned and marched down the road, silent and sure, the way she did everything. Dave wasn't sure if he should go after her or call this the end. He really didn't want to do that though, so he jogged after her and caught up to her.

"Look," he said, calmer and in a gentler tone. "Sissy, can you wait?" He reached out and touched her arm.

She froze, her glare hot and angry.

Dave fell back a step, unsure of what to do now. "Look," he said again, the words building beneath his tongue. "I'm in love with you, okay?" He exhaled like being in love was a horrible thing to be. "I love you. And I'm just—so frustrated that I'm here again, when you're obviously not, and I don't want to go to your mother's and pretend like we're okay when we're obviously not."

He breathed, the load he'd been carrying around with him for weeks suddenly gone.

"I love you too," she said, and Dave's eyes flew to hers. Her voice sounded tinny and far away, and tears gathered in her eyes.

He shook his head. "No, sweetheart. You don't. You love the *idea* of me. The *idea* of us. Like, oh it's so great I got my second chance." The bitterness crept into his voice and his soul, and he didn't like it. Pushed against it.

"The thing is, Sissy, I know what being loved by you feels like." He gestured between the two of them. "And this isn't it."

That was the raw truth, and he hated how it sounded, but it was what it was. True.

She did want a family. A husband. But at the same time, she didn't.

Dave felt himself falling, much the same way he had when she'd broken up with him the first time. The difference now was, he was going to be the one to end things with her.

Give her a way out.

That was the thought that had been in his mind since the rodeo, since he'd known he was in love with her all over again. She might be content running on the hamster wheel and kissing him whenever she felt like it.

But he wasn't.

He wanted more. He wanted *her* to commit to *him*. Run to him instead of away from him. Take him home to show him off because she loved him, not because she wanted to prove something to her sister and her mom.

Tears splashed her face, and Dave wanted to wipe them away. Kiss it all better. Promise her forever.

Instead, he said, "I think we both know we're done." He waited for her to contradict him, but she didn't. She just stood there, crying, Then she nodded, turned, and walked away from him.

DAVE WATCHED Sissy drive off the ranch a couple of hours later. He couldn't see her face, and he hated that he was skulking in the shadows near the chicken coop— mostly because the smell there wasn't great, especially in the near-July heat.

He'd done a few chores in the llama barn after he'd ended things with Sissy, and then he'd taken up a post to make sure he knew when she was gone.

Relief and disappointment married inside him, and they created odd bedfellows. He felt upside down when he was right-side up, but he managed to get back to his cabin. He stood in the living room, looking around, his thoughts spinning out of control.

Should he leave? Would she quit? Or could they go back to the way it had been for the two years they'd worked together and never spoken to one another?

In all honestly, Dave thought Sissy would run again, so when she didn't show up for work the next day, he wasn't all that surprised. Of course, it was a Saturday, but she didn't text him or ask him to come down for lunch or a quick trip to some shop she wanted to visit. They spent weekends together, doing things in Pasadena and attending church, walking around the ranch and sharing their lives.

But that weekend, he spent his Saturday catching up on chores he hadn't done the day before, and his Sunday alone on the bench in the chapel. He didn't see Sissy, and he knew she'd left town. Gone to her mother's for the Tuesday holiday, and Dave didn't think she'd be back.

He wanted to go ask Scarlett, but he didn't want to be that guy. So he kept his head down and disappeared inside his cabin after church, ignored the text for lunch on Monday, and went to set up for the Fourth of July picnic the way he'd agreed to do.

The activity around the ranch, as well as the jovial mood, helped to lift him out of the funk he'd fallen into. He'd been here before; he knew what to do.

Keep breathing in and out. Try to stop thinking about Sissy, and where Sissy had gone, and if she'd posted on her social media. That way, at least he'd be able to stop obsessing over her for at least a couple of days.

Then he'd have to check again.

Today, he knew she was in San Diego, at her mother's. Probably eating potato salad and hot dogs, like most of the rest of the country. Like he'd be doing in about an hour.

He kept breathing. He got the tent set up, and chairs put at the tables. He carried what Scarlett told him to carry, and he bowed his head while Carson said grace.

He loaded his plate with food and sat beside Cache and Lance while Sawyer held his baby so Jeri could eat first. Soon enough, he passed Brayden to Jeri, and Sawyer filled a plate with a burger and chips, salads and dips and fruit, as if he hadn't eaten in weeks.

Dave attempted to be present, and he thought he did a decent job. Forever Friends had sponsored a huge fireworks display at the church at the bottom of the bluff, and they had several employees there to do dog and cat adoptions.

He helped load animals into carriers and trucks to be taken down to the event, and he saw Lance flirting with Amber as they set up tables for food and adoption paperwork. Kaylee was obviously a distant memory, and Dave knew Amber had broken up with the volunteer.

And now it looked like Lance wasn't going to miss his chance. Normally, Dave would've been happy for the usually shy, reserved cowboy, and Dave *did* feel happy for him.

He also had an incredible, raging river of jealousy flowing through him. So strongly, he actually paused and watched Lance touch her hand and pull back, a smile on his face, trying to remember how to breathe.

Spinning away, he set down the cat carrier in his hand and walked away. He wanted to run, the way Sissy always seemed to be able to do. Pack a bag, load up in his truck, and just go. Desperation filled his throat, and he clenched his teeth to keep his anger from exploding out in a yell.

Why did this have to happen again? he asked God, desperate to know the answer. Desperate to know if he'd just been hung up on the wrong woman for his entire life. The thought felt false, and he remembered all the good times they'd had going to church together.

"Then why can't this work out like it does in the movies?" he whispered. "Please." He didn't want to beg, but he figured if there was anyone to plead with in a situation like this, it was the Lord.

"Dave," Hudson called, and Dave swung around to see him gesturing for him to come help. So Dave did what he'd done last time Sissy had taken his heart and choked it to death. He went back to work. At least this time it was to help Hudson with a couple of dogs and not off to war again.

Friendly dogs, who just had a little too much energy, and Dave kept a good hold on their leashes while Hudson turned to another task. "Let's go, guys," he said to the pups. If they got some energy out, they'd be better during the dinner and subsequent fireworks. Plus, it gave Dave an excuse to run away for a little bit.

He walked briskly, keeping the dogs right at his side. They did what they wanted, though they both tried to pull more than once. About twenty minutes down the path, they finally settled into submission, both of them panting.

Dave wished he'd brought Stella, but she was a bit skittish around loud noises, and she was just as happy to sleep on his bed as she was to lay by him while the fireworks went off. By the time he made it back to the setup at the church, there were dozens of people there. Some throwing balls to dogs. Some walking them. Some looking at the cats. Most eating the hamburgers and hot dogs three volunteers from Forever Friends were serving up with smiles.

A little boy came over and asked, "Can I pat your dog?"

"Sure," Dave said, the child's enthusiasm hard to ignore. He made both dogs sit down, and then he allowed the boy to give them a good pat. They were obedient, and the black and white mutt seemed to smile right up at the boy. He called his mother over, and Dave passed the leash to him with the words, "He can pull a little, but I tired him out for you."

He kept hold of the gray pit bull and took him with him as he went through the food line to get dinner. He sat beside Karla and Cache with the words, "I'm not interrupting, am I?"

"Nope," Karla said, her voice a bit abrupt. Dave glanced at her, the marketing director who'd taken Last Chance Ranch off the bluff and onto the Internet. Their horseback riding lessons had tripled in the time Karla had been working at the ranch, and they had nightly goat yoga now too. She organized tours, and part of her salary was paid by Forever Friends, and she did a ton for them too.

Dave looked at Cache, who couldn't seem to look anywhere but at his food. He'd definitely interrupted, but he'd rather be here with this couple that wasn't getting along than with the happier ones who couldn't seem to keep their hands to themselves.

He felt sick to his stomach, and he didn't want to be there. "I'm sorry," he said, getting up. "I have to go."

"Go?" Cache said after him, but Dave was already walking away, taking the gray bull dog with him. He didn't know the dog's name, but he could sleep with him and Stella, no problem.

At least he wouldn't be completely alone this time.

Chapter Nineteen

S issy texted Scarlett about needing a few days off to go visit family, and the ranch owner hadn't bought it for a second. Sissy hadn't really believed she would. But she'd packed a bag and asked Clara to please come feed her cat and take the parakeet back to her place so it wouldn't die of loneliness.

Clara had laughed at her, but Sissy knew birds could pine for their owners and actually die. She also knew what it felt like to want to die from loneliness. She'd never been all that great at being alone. Being stationary.

Even when she'd come to Pasadena and got a house and started a more permanent job at the ranch, she'd made quick friends and dated a lot. She didn't want to go home to her house by herself.

She couldn't believe Dave had broken up with her. Couldn't believe he loved her.

"Of course you believe that," she told herself as she heaved her suitcase into the back of her car. Though she was overweight and wore the wrong shoes around the ranch, Dave loved her. On some level, he'd always loved her. She'd felt it in his touch. In the way he kissed her. The simple way he looked at her.

Why couldn't she love him back the way he needed her to?

Tears came to her eyes, and her frustration with herself rose and rose. She thought it would eventually peak, but it didn't. Just kept building and building until she had to pull off the freeway so she could let it all out.

Sitting in her car, somewhere between the life she wanted and her mother's house, Sissy sobbed and sobbed.

"What do I do now?" she begged the Lord. "Why am I like this?"

Eventually her crying subsided, and a sense of calmness came over her. She drew in one deep breath and then another. "Okay," she said. "All right." She gripped the steering wheel. "Help me here, Jesus." Wasn't there a song about letting the Lord take the wheel? She knew how to get to her mother's house. She knew how to find her way home. How to get to the ranch, do her job, and make friends.

What she didn't know how to do was navigate her own feelings and allow herself to love Dave Merrill.

"I *do* love him, though," she whispered. The thought of not being with him made fresh tears prick her eyes. The idea of him being with someone else made her fingers tighten on that wheel.

All at once, she let go, lifting her hands up into the air. "I can't do this on my own. Tell me what to do."

No immediate answer came to mind, but Sissy felt calm enough to continue her journey toward her mother's house. She wouldn't be arriving that day, though she could easily make the drive. In fact, she didn't drive very much farther at all. Just through the city to Huntington Beach, where she found a hotel and checked herself in.

Though she was curvy, with dozens of extra pounds on her, she didn't mind how she looked in a bathing suit. She adored laying on the beach and listening to the waves roll in, so she spent the afternoon behind mirrored sunglasses, crying occasionally and eating too much junk food as she tried to find a way to fix what she'd done.

Could she just call Dave? Apologize?

That almost felt too easy, and she didn't think he'd take her back anyway. "You hurt him," she whispered to the summer sun as it arced toward the ocean. "You hurt him *again*."

The following day was the Sabbath, and while she didn't usually seek out a church and attend if she was traveling, today she did. She found a little white church a few blocks from her hotel, and she donned a cute yellow sundress and left her hair to fall over her shoulders as preparation to go.

Her nerves danced through her system as she walked

inside. There was something a little frightening about going somewhere new and having to talk to new people, explain she was just a visitor, and try to feel something too.

But Sissy made it onto a bench on the side without any interaction, and she sat with her hands resting easily in her lap as she gazed at the beautiful stained glass window behind the dais. She hadn't seen this window from the front of the building, and the way the sunlight illuminated the scene from the garden of Gethsemane touched her heart.

Tears flowed down her face before she could stop them, and she was eternally grateful she'd decided to go plain today. No makeup. No jewelry. She looked like she'd just walked in off the beach, but a couple went past her to the row a few in front of her, and that woman wasn't even wearing a skirt. They were probably visitors too, and Sissy was glad she'd come.

Glad others felt like they could come wearing whatever they had with them. Glad God accepted all people into his houses of worship. The pastor got up, and Sissy looked at him, marveling at how young he was.

"Welcome, everyone," he said. "I see several new faces, and whether you're new to our little flock or just passing through, we're glad you're here."

Sissy could feel his general happiness from her spot near the back, and for some reason, that touched her heart.

"Have you ever felt like the journey you're on is too long?" he asked next, and Sissy jerked her attention back to him. She did feel like that. "Too many steps, with so many obstacles to overcome? What do you do in those situations? Give up? Plow forward? Move off onto a side path?"

He gave some examples of situations where someone might feel like that—a dead end job, trying to finish school, or simply trudging through everyday life, especially after the loss of a loved one.

Sissy marveled at the rich, smooth way he delivered his sermon, at how sure he was about seemingly everything. She also liked that he didn't tell the people exactly what to do. Instead he said, "Sometimes it's okay to give up. Sometimes God is pushing you toward a side path. And sometimes, He's testing us to see if we'll push through and come out triumphant on the other side."

Sissy stayed in her seat for a few minutes after the sermon ended, watching others as they left the chapel. But she wanted to stay and think, and she hoped that would be okay. The chatter in the lobby behind her quieted, and Sissy closed her eyes to pray.

Thoughts streamed through her mind, and she let them talk and go wherever they wanted.

You've had your side path, one said.

Don't give up, another said.

What's on the other side? a third asked.

Sissy knew what was on the other side. The house with the white picket fence. Dave beside her when she woke up. A baby in the nursery.

Happiness and joy.

Love and kindness, without loneliness or heartache.

Sure, she knew things wouldn't always be new babies and horseback riding into the sunset. But she knew she didn't want to go back to Last Chance Ranch and not be able to talk to Dave. She didn't want to go back to blind dates at Scooter's while her friends vetted the man as they brought him to the table.

She didn't want to be the woman she'd been all those years ago when she'd given Dave his diamond and hopped on the next flight out of town.

She wanted to plow through.

Excited at this breakthrough in her own mind, she stood up to leave the chapel. The pastor stood at the back of the room, watching her, and she said, "I'm sorry I stayed so long," as she approached him.

"The chapel is always open," he said with a smile. "Visiting today?"

"Yes," she said. "That was one of the best sermons I've heard in a long time."

"Thank you," he said simply. "Where do you call home?"

"I'm in Pasadena," she said. "I work at a rescue ranch there."

"Oh, my brother's in that area."

"Really?" she asked. "What a small world. What does he do?"

"He's at the rescue ranch there, too. Last Chance Ranch, isn't it?"

Sissy froze, trying to remember all of Dave's brothers. He did have two—one older and one younger—but she couldn't see any Merrill features in this man. "Who is it?"

"Ames Golden," he said with a smile.

"Oh, I know Ames," she said, a rush of relief painting her insides. "He's a great guy."

The pastor chuckled. "That he is. Tell him I said hello."

"I sure will."

He grinned again and headed down the hall, leaving the path for Sissy to leave the church wide open. She did, and though it was hot, she wandered down the street to find something to eat. Then she hit the beach again, the notebook app on her phone open so she could type in any thoughts that came about how to plow through and get to the other side of this difficult path she was on.

Not much came, and all she typed in was *apologize* before the time came that she needed to get back to the hotel.

Another day passed where nothing more came to mind. She was set to leave Huntington Beach on the morning of the Fourth, but putting more distance between her and Dave felt like the wrong thing to do.

She texted her mother that she wouldn't be coming after all, and her mom called her instantly.

"What's going on?" she asked by way of hello.

"I'm just...not in a good place for a picnic," Sissy said, gazing out her hotel window. She only had an hour left to get out, and she hadn't started packing yet. She once again felt stuck, this time without Dave's shoulder to lean on.

"Did something happen with Dave?"

Sissy began crying, and she wouldn't be able to hide it from her mother. "I don't know what's wrong with me, Mom," she said through the tears. "He loves me, and I just...." She couldn't continue, and she hated that she wasn't enough for him.

"You broke up with him again," her mom said.

"No," Sissy said, swiping at her tears and making her voice strong. "He broke up with me. Says we're just spinning our wheels, and he thinks maybe I'll never come around."

"What is taking you so long to come around, Sis? You've loved this man for decades."

"I know." And she did love him. On so many levels. But the one he deserved, she didn't.

"So what is it?"

"I don't know."

"That's rubbish," her mom said, adopting some of her boyfriend's way of talking. "I don't believe that for a second. Just say whatever comes to your mind. Why can't you be with him?"

"Because," Sissy said. "He's better than me. He loves me more than I love him, and that's not fair." She sucked in a breath, full realization hitting her then.

"Who says you have to love each other equally?" her mom asked.

"I have to go," Sissy said. "I'm sorry, Mom. I'll call you later." She hung up and spun back to her suitcase. She had to pack. Packing now. She could do that.

Then she had to get back to Last Chance Ranch and do a few things before she talked to Dave.

The idea of coming face-to-face with him and vocalizing some of her deepest fears had her hands trembling, but she could push through it.

She had to.

She would.

"I can," she told herself as she zipped her suitcase closed and headed for the door.

Chapter Twenty

David ended up on his back porch with both dogs, watching the fireworks. Stella barked and tried to climb into Dave's lap every so often, but the pit bull just laid beside him, panting.

He normally loved the Fourth, the spirit of patriotism, and a general feeling that he'd served his country well. His weekend at the base was only a few days away, and he knew they'd celebrate there too.

Everything felt hollow now, like he'd lost an essential part of himself. Another firework spit red sparks into the sky, the boom coming a moment later. Stella barked, and he quieted her. But the pit bull got to his feet too, turning back to the house. The dogs looked at each other and trotted into the house, Stella barking loudly now.

"It's just the fireworks, guys," he said, peering over his shoulder. Everyone on the ranch had gone down to the

193

field beside the church to participate in the festivities. Dave could feel the emptiness on the ranch, feel the emptiness way down deep inside himself.

Should I call Sissy? he wondered, trying to find the center of himself and listen to it. God had never directed him incorrectly, but he sort of felt like the Lord had put him on a boat in the middle of a raging sea. "It sure would be nice to see someone walking toward me right now," he murmured. "Calming the storm."

He'd loved the Bible stories growing up, and the ones with the Savior in them were his favorite. But the storm raged on, and Dave clung to the side of the boat as three fireworks popped overhead, one red, one white, and one blue.

How very patriotic.

Stella barked again, this time coming back to the door and looking at him like, *Come on, cowboy. I need you in here.*

"What is it?" he asked, finally getting up and going inside. He didn't see anything out of the ordinary—except for the gray pit bull standing in an inch from the front door. "Is someone there?"

Stella did a half-trot, half-gallop over to the door too, just as someone knocked on it. Someone *was* there.

"Odd," Dave said as he strode through his cabin.

"Dave?" a woman called, and he froze. Not just any woman.

Sissy was here.

Sissy's here, his mind whispered, the two words starting to echo around inside his mind until they became a scream. *Sissy's here. Sissy's here. Sissy's here!*

She knocked again, and Dave felt himself rip right down the middle. He wanted to hurry the rest of the way to the door and yank it open. Gather her into his arms. Tell her he loved her and would wait for however long she needed.

The other half wanted to go quickly back to the back porch and pretend he hadn't heard her knocking.

Something creaked on the other side of the door, and he recognized the sound of his front steps. Specifically the last one before the porch. So she'd left.

But she came back, the excited voice in his mind said, *Go talk to her. Just see what she has to say.*

He moved, but not in a rush. He opened the front door amidst whining from Stella, and both dogs rushed out onto the porch before he could even get the door open all the way.

Sissy giggled from her position on the top step, and said, "Oh, hello, Stella," as the dog licked her face. "And who are you? Did Dave get a new dog?" She twisted to look over her shoulder just as Dave settled into the doorway, mostly to keep himself from rushing toward her and doing the kissing and apologizing.

She'd come to him. Four long days she'd stayed away.

But she'd come back.

"Hey." She pushed the dogs away and stood up,

smoothing her palms down the front of her shorts. Her smile had disappeared, and she wore all that beautiful, dark hair up in a ponytail high on her head.

"Hey," he said back. If she was here to further injure him, he didn't know what he'd do. He reminded himself that Sissy wasn't like that. She wasn't intentionally unkind or cruel. She just...had a gypsy spirit. One that couldn't be contained. It was actually something he really loved about her.

"I saw your truck, and I was sort of surprised you weren't down at the Forever Friends thing."

"Yeah," he said, because he didn't know what else to say. Questions piled up in his throat, but he held them back. *She* had come to *him*, and she very clearly had something to say. He'd said everything on the road a few days ago anyway.

She glanced away, into the darkness beyond his front porch, and then looked at him again. Tucking her hands in her back pockets, she took a step toward him. Dave's attraction to her shot off the charts, but he maintained his position in the doorway, both dogs now at his feet.

"I just...." She inhaled and exhaled heavily. "I want to plow through with you."

Confusion touched his mind. "What?"

She stilled a few feet from him, but she was so close he could see she wasn't wearing any makeup, and the scent of her filled the air. Something like sunshine and strawberries and the minty chapstick she liked to wear.

He liked her in her natural form, and everything male in him wanted her in his arms as soon as possible. He watched her struggle to come up with the right words, and he waited.

"I went to this church in Huntington Beach a couple of days ago," she said, her voice raw and tense. "And I'm not perfect, but you're not perfect either. I think what's holding me back from being with you is that I think I have to be perfect to love you. That you expect me to love you perfectly." She cleared her throat. "And I don't, and while I want to, I'm not there yet."

He had no idea what she was saying, but he'd heard the word *love* a few times. He wasn't sure if she was saying she did love him or she didn't.

"But I want to plow through all of that. I *do* love you, and I want to be with you. I want the house with you. I want the family with you. I want to go to sleep with you at my side, and I want to wake up with you singing those cowboy songs in the shower." She half laughed and half cried, her tears shining under the porch light while the fireworks continued to explode behind the house.

Dave's whole heart filled with love for her. "I don't sing in the shower," he said, and she burst out laughing.

He couldn't keep the smile off his face and the hope out of his heart. No, things weren't perfect between them. She'd left—but she'd *come back*. Sissy had never come back to him before.

She quieted as she wiped the tears from her face. "Dave, I'm so sorry. Can you forgive me twice?"

"I can forgive you as many times as it takes," he whispered, and she flew into his arms. Her shoulders shook as she cried, and Dave just held her, trying to keep everything inside him from storming out too.

"I love you," she said through her tears, and Dave whispered it back to her just before he kissed her.

AN HOUR LATER, the fireworks show had ended. Trucks and cars had returned to the ranch. He and Sissy had stayed on the back porch, their hands entwined as they talked and sat with the dogs.

"Did you really adopt another dog?"

"Not yet," he said. "I don't even know this one's name."

Sissy shook her head. "He just followed you home, is that it?"

"He was supposed to be down at the adoption event," Dave said, realizing he'd probably kept the dog from getting adopted. "He had a little too much energy, so I took him for a walk."

"Why weren't you down there? Seems like your kind of scene."

"Yeah," he said. "I tried." He didn't want to say any more. If Sissy didn't already know the great hold she had over his heart, he didn't need to spell it out for her. Make himself appear even more pathetic.

Falling in love wasn't pathetic, he knew. It was a gift, and he mentally thanked the Lord for giving Sissy a way back to him. She'd told him all about the sermon and what she'd learned about herself.

He didn't know how to reassure her that he loved her completely for the person she was. Not the person she'd been. Not who he hoped she could be in the future. But the kind, generous, hardworking, gorgeous woman she was right now.

He squeezed her hand and said, "I'm glad you came back. I was going to go talk to Scarlett tomorrow and offer to quit."

Sissy leaned her head against his bicep and sighed. "I would've been mortified to drive you away from this ranch you love so much."

Dave felt a sense of peace enter his heart. "Well, I don't have to do that now, do I?"

"No," she whispered.

"Can we live in your place in town once we get married?" he asked.

Sissy lifted her head from his shoulder. "Is that a proposal?"

He chuckled and shook his head. "No, sweetheart. That was not a proposal." He looked at her. "You want to get married, right?" She'd said she wanted the house, the family, and him at her side. Maybe that didn't mean marriage.

"Of course," she said.

"When?" he asked.

She looked at him, her dark eyes sparking with an emotion he couldn't name. "I don't know."

"You never thought about it?" he asked. "Last time, I believe you said you wanted a spring wedding."

"I don't think things like that are as important anymore," she said.

"Fascinating."

Sissy grinned at him. "And I think I'll ask you this time. So you decide when we get married."

"You are not asking me," he said, keeping his gaze out into the darkness where the gray pit bull had disappeared a few minutes ago. He wasn't worried about the dog; it would come back.

"Why not?"

"Because." Dave didn't need to get into all the reasons he didn't like that idea.

"Dave—"

"Because I already have a ring for you," he said, meeting her gaze.

Surprise danced across her face. "You do?"

"Yes."

"I want to see it."

Of course she did. Dave sighed like she was doing something terrible, but he pushed into a stand. "Fine." He went inside and down the hall to his bedroom, his heart beating quicker with every step. In his top dresser drawer, way in the back, he pulled out the black box her first engagement ring had come in.

Would she think him stupid for keeping it all these years? *Was* he stupid for doing so? He'd come to the ranch without knowing Sissy worked here, and he'd had the ring then. Maybe it was romantic.

He didn't have flowers. He didn't have balloons or candlelight. He didn't have a catered dinner on the beach.

He just had himself, and at this point in his life, it had to be enough. *He* was enough.

Back outside, he sat down beside her again, noting the pit bull had returned, and handed her the box silently.

She looked at it and then him before returning her attention to it. As she cracked the lid, Dave's pulse nearly exploded through his veins, so much like the fireworks a few minutes ago had burst into the sky.

Sissy sucked in a breath and started crying all in the same second.

"I can get a better one," he said. "I have more money now. You can pick it out."

"No," she said, still staring down at the simple gold band with the small diamond in it that he'd bought for her eighteen years ago. "It's perfect." She looked at him with those joyful, watery eyes, and Dave had never felt such love from her. She truly loved him, and in that moment, he knew it.

"Will you marry me?" he asked. Not down on one knee. Just sitting beside her on the back porch, like he wanted to do every night before they went to bed.

"Yes," she whispered, leaning over to kiss him. The sweet, gentle movement of her mouth against his made this kiss with his fiancée one of the best of his life.

"Let me put it on," he said, pulling away. He slipped the simple ring on her finger, and she held her hand out for them both to see.

"I love it."

Dave did too. It was more than just an engagement ring. It was a symbol of everything they'd been through together.

"Let's talk about a date in the morning," he said with a yawn. "I'm exhausted."

She agreed, and he walked her through the cabin to her car in the driveway, where he kissed her and stood in the road while her taillights left the ranch. He didn't like that, and he wanted to get married as soon as possible so she didn't have to drive away from him at night.

I'll talk to her in the morning, he told himself as he went back inside the cabin to find both dogs already on his bed.

Chapter Twenty-One

Sissy found Dave's truck parked next to the administration building when she pulled in the next morning. He sat on the steps in front of the glass doors, his cowboy hat hiding his face as he looked at his phone.

When she got out, he looked up and then stood up. "Morning, sweetheart." He leaned down and kissed her, his cowboy hat falling to the gravel at their feet. "I've been thinking."

"Oh, sounds dangerous." She stooped to get his hat, setting it on his head. "I've been thinking too."

He straightened his hat. "You go first. Then I'll know what to say."

She went up the steps, pulling her keys to the building from her purse. "Okay, but I just want to say it, and you can tell me I'm crazy or not afterward."

"I can do that." He held the door for her as she went in, following behind her.

Sissy's mouth turned dry. But she'd been up for hours, texting her mother and then her girlfriends. She went into her office and put her purse down before turning back to Dave, who'd paused in the doorway. "I want to get married as soon as possible."

He stood there and stared at her. Several moments passed while her heart beat out of her chest. Had he changed his mind? She swept her arms out in front of her. "That's all. That's what I've been thinking about."

"Oh," he said. "I thought you said I had to wait until you were done, and I thought there'd be more." He ducked his head, and when he lifted it again, he wore a sexy, cowboy smile.

"That's what I've been thinking too," he said, taking a slow step toward her. "I wasn't kidding when I said I'd marry you tomorrow and get to work on those babies."

Sissy's whole body filled with heat. "I'd like a couple of weeks to put a few things together. Nothing big."

"You're sure?" he asked. "You've never been married. You don't want the everything?"

"Oh, I want everything," she said. "But I've already been talking to my mom, and we think we can do everything and have a beautiful wedding with our friends and family in a month."

"A month," Dave repeated. "So we're talking August."

"August tenth," she said. "It's a Friday, and I need to

talk to Scarlett, but my mom's not working that weekend, and that gives her and Jessie time to come. My dad and his new wife will want to be here." She rolled her eyes. "But yes. It's thirty-five days." She swallowed, the tasks in front of her daunting to say the least.

"I suppose I can live without you for thirty-five more days," he said.

"You're not without me," she said, slightly confused.

"Oh, but I am." He moved right into her personal space, swept her into his arms, and kissed her. Just as quickly as he'd done that, he stepped back, leaving Sissy woozy and slightly disoriented.

"Okay." She patted her hair, because he'd ran his fingers through it, and stepped around her desk. "Thirty-five days."

"Thirty-five days," he repeated. He touched the brim of his hat, smiled, and said, "See you later."

With him gone, Sissy collapsed in her desk chair, a wide smile stealing across her face. A word ran through her mind, one she hadn't truly thought of before.

Wife.

She couldn't wait to be his wife.

———

"THEY'RE MEANT to echo wildflowers, Mom," Sissy said a week later. "That's what I want. We're getting married on a ranch. We don't need a zillion roses in ten different colors." She ran a washcloth over the table where her friends would be gathering in a couple of hours. "So I'm happy with them."

Not only that, but the florist she'd talked to could deliver them on time.

"As long as you're happy," her mom said, but it didn't really sound like that was true. Sissy had decided she didn't care. Yes, she needed her mother's help, but she herself was paying for everything. So if Sissy wanted the smaller, simpler bouquet, that was what she was going to get.

"Did you get pictures taken?"

"Yes, just last night," she said. "She said she'd rush them, so I can get announcements out." She hadn't even wanted to do announcements. They felt dated and old-fashioned, but her mother had insisted.

"You'll want something to remember the event with," she'd said. Sissy thought wedding day pictures would be enough. She had social media; she could alert those she cared about. Besides that, all of those people knew already. It had finally come out that her mother wanted Sissy to send the announcement to her father and his parents, as if they wouldn't attend the wedding without a formal, printed, and mailed announcement.

"And the cake?"

"Karla is going to make it," she said. "And I'm going shopping for the dress again this weekend." Things had come together fairly fast and all the parts of a wedding had solidified pretty easily.

Venue. Check. Flowers. Check. Cake. Check. Guests. Check. Groom. Check.

She just needed a dress.

"Do you want me to come help with the dress?" her mother asked, and Sissy paused in her cleaning of the kitchen. The very real feeling like her mother wanted to come spread through her, and while Sissy was more than capable of going shopping herself, or taking one of her girl-friends, she said, "I thought you had to work this weekend."

"I can take it off," her mom said.

"Then yes," Sissy said quickly. "I'd love to have you come help me find my wedding dress."

"Great," her mom said, her voice pitched much too high. "I'll see you Friday night." The call ended almost immediately after that, and Sissy wept silently as she finished cleaning up her kitchen.

"Thank you, Lord," she whispered, so much to be grateful for.

The weeks passed, and it took her mother driving to LA for two weekends in a row before Sissy found the just-right dress that she could afford at one of the boutiques in the city. Her mother had actually found it, and Sissy may or may not have buttoned herself into the dress every night since purchasing it.

And now, she just had to wear it one more time to become David Merrill's wife.

Her nerves shot through her like cannons, and she couldn't hold still while Kirsten pinned up another lock of her hair. "Girl," her friend said, letting the piece back down.

"I'm trying," Sissy said. "I'm just so nervous."

"Why?" Clara said, moving in front of her with the foundation again. Sissy had specifically said not to put on too much make-up, but Clara seemed to have developed selective hearing as Sissy already wore false eyelashes.

"I don't know," she admitted.

"It's Dave," Hailey said as she came in with another flower arrangement. "And these boutonnieres are gorgeous. Who am I walking down the aisle with again?"

"Ames," Sissy said.

"I can't believe you stuck me with Gray," Kirsten said, pulling a bit too hard on Sissy's hair.

"Hey, he's totally your type," Sissy said.

"Really?" Their eyes met in the mirror. "You made him sound like a conceited, arrogant cowboy. That's my type?"

Sissy just smiled at Kirsten. She did like the fussier men, and Gray never went anywhere without being pressed and polished and perfect. They'd look great together, and she closed her eyes as Clara leaned in to put powder on her face.

"At least you didn't get a throwaway," Clara said.

"Cache has a girlfriend he's just not talking to at the moment."

"They broke up," Sissy said. "He doesn't have a girlfriend."

"Right," Clara said. "Didn't Dave say he'd be shocked if they weren't back together by the wedding?" The brush went swish, swish, swish across Sissy's face. She wished she hadn't had Dave over for dinner with her girlfriends. But he'd wanted to meet them all, and as these were the two most important halves of her life, she'd merged them.

She'd just need to tell him that, in the future, he couldn't give away any cowboy secrets from the ranch.

"Scarlett just hired someone new," Sissy said. "I can switch him and Cache, if you want."

"What's his name?"

"Cook."

"His first name."

"That is his first name. Cook Winchester."

Clara scoffed and the brush disappeared from Sissy's face. "That's the most ridiculous name I've ever heard."

"So I'll switch him and Cache."

"All right," Clara said off-hand, like she didn't care. But she clearly did. And then Karla and Cache could walk down the aisle together, and maybe they could make up. They were cute together, and Sissy thought they probably just needed to work through a few things the way she had. Then they'd have their own wedding at Last Chance Ranch.

When she was buffed and pinned and brushed, she piled in the car with her friends, and they drove her up to the ranch. The huge tents they used for the ranch-wide picnics had been set up in the field just east of the administration building. Her mother's car was already parked there, and she and Jessie emerged from the building as Sissy got out of the car.

She held her skirts up so they wouldn't drag in the dirt and hurried up the steps when her mom said, "Dave is almost ready. His mother just left to go take her seat."

Sissy nodded and went inside the building and ducked into the first room on her right. A conference room they never used, her mother had set up their main operations there. Piles of napkins and plates waited on the table.

"Everything went okay with the decorating?" she asked. The wedding would take place outside, but the reception and dinner would be right here, in this building. With everyone who worked at the ranch, plus her family and Dave's, they were feeding seventy-five people.

"Didn't you see the table when you came in?" her mother asked.

Sissy hadn't, so she stepped back over to the door and looked out into the expansive foyer. A huge flower arrangement had been set on the center table, and beside that, a picture of her and Dave. Their engagement picture.

A book lay next to that, and Sissy smiled. "It's perfect, Mom."

"So people can write you a message," she said. "And

then go down the hall to eat. We'll come back out here to cut the cake and do the dancing."

"You think there's enough room?" Sissy had worried about it for weeks. She didn't need a formal dinner and dancing, but Scarlett had offered her full use of the ranch. She and Adele had gotten married here on the ranch as well, but they'd had their after parties in the barn.

Sissy wasn't the barn-loving type, and she'd opted for the place where she worked all day long.

"There's plenty of room," her mother assured her. "Let me fix that strap, and then we better go take our seats too. Your dad will be here any minute." She stepped over and lovingly tucked and smoothed part of Sissy's dress along her shoulder.

"You're stunning, darling." She pressed a kiss to her cheek, and she and Jessie bustled out of the building and across the street. Sissy moved to the window and watched as several more people arrived and got out of their cars. The tent appeared to be full, but she couldn't really tell from here.

She wrung her hands, wishing she'd asked someone else to walk her down the aisle. She wasn't particularly close with her father, and she'd been a bit surprised when he'd accepted.

"Sissy," a man said, and she turned to find her father filling the doorway

"Daddy." She hurried over to him, smiling and weeping at the same time. She didn't want someone else to walk her down the aisle anymore, as he hugged her tight and whispered how much he loved her.

Maybe there was more to say. Or maybe it was just that easy to forgive someone she cared about. No matter what, she said, "I love you too, Dad," and straightened her dress so she'd be flawless when it was finally her turn to walk down the aisle.

Chapter Twenty-Two

Dave thought Sissy would never be ready. He worried she'd gotten cold feet and fled the state. He stood at the altar with Ames's brother—the pastor who'd spoken to Sissy's heart and soul in Huntington Beach, his eyes glued to the other end of the aisle.

Everyone seemed to be in position. Her family, minus her dad, had come in several minutes ago and taken their seats on the front row. All the bridesmaids and groomsmen waited in line just outside the tent. He couldn't see past them, and that was the whole point. Sissy didn't want him to see her until she was almost to the altar.

She'd asked everyone and their cowboy to be in the wedding party, and he'd done whatever she'd asked him to over the last thirty-five days. She needed something picked up in town? He could do that. She needed him to stay home so she could go shopping with her mom? He'd done it. She wanted his opinion on what to serve for their wedding dinner? He'd eaten and sampled and given his opinion.

But all he really wanted was her to walk down the aisle and say "I do."

Just when he was about to stride out of the tent and find her, a murmur lifted into the air. The bridesmaids and groomsmen at the end of the aisle straightened up, and the music began to play from the speakers Hudson and Scarlett had set up. They were pros at outdoor weddings, as this was the fourth one on the ranch in the last few years.

People moved, and he grinned at Sawyer, and Cache, and Lance.

Finally, Sissy and her dad came into view. She wore a strappy dress that flowed around her body like water, with her dark hair all pinned up with pearls. The fabric seemed like it was made more of air than anything, and the glorious smile on her face stole his breath away.

Her dad leaned over and kissed her forehead before passing her to Dave, who could only stare at her, dumbfounded.

She'd shown up.

And she was beautiful. She was his.

He kept her arm tight against his as they faced the pastor. He felt inadequate to be her husband, but he knew she struggled with similar feelings about being his wife. They'd work on it together.

"What a joyous occasion," Pastor Golden started, the happiness on his face and in his voice absolutely infectious. "To see two people pledging their lives to one another always brings my soul such joy. Today, we celebrate the love and life of David Merrill and Cecily Longston." He continued with his speech, promising peace and love to everyone if they simply followed their hearts and listened to the Lord.

Dave could see why Sissy had liked him so much. When he said, "Cecily, do you promise to love, honor, and respect David?" she gave the right answer.

And when it was his turn, he said in a loud, clear voice, "I do."

"I now pronounce you husband and wife." Pastor Golden grinned. "Let's see a kiss."

Dave grinned at Sissy, happier than he'd ever been. Surely this life couldn't get any better, no matter where they went or what they did. He held onto Sissy and kissed her like a man in love with her.

Because that was what he was.

SISSY WOULDN'T STOP CRYING, and Dave didn't know what to do about it. He'd told himself over and over that it was fine. She was allowed to cry over things. Hard things and happy things.

"We're here," he said when he pulled into the parking

lot at the hospital. Neither of them made a move to get out. "You still want to do this, right?"

Because adoption wasn't cheap, and their whole lives were about to change.

"Yes." She strengthened her shoulders and wiped her eyes. "I want this so much." She looked at him, her face crumbling again.

He'd asked her before why she cried when she was happy, but she'd said she didn't know. He'd learned over the past six months that it was just a release for her. A release for good emotions, and for bad.

"Come on, then," he said as he got out of the car. They held hands on the way in, Sissy clenching his so tight, he thought he might lose feeling in it. The birth mother they'd been talking to for three months had gone into labor last night.

She hadn't wanted anyone there with her. Not her mother. Not her boyfriend. Not even Sissy and Dave.

He'd been praying with everything he had that she hadn't changed her mind. That the baby was healthy. That everything had gone well. He had no reason to believe anything would be wrong, but she was only seventeen years old, and Dave couldn't help the nerves and worry streaming through him.

He pushed the button to go up to the maternity ward and said, "Do you want to text her that we're here?"

"Yes." Sissy removed her hand from Dave's and started texting Lola. By the time the elevator spit them out on the fourth floor, Sissy said, "She's ready for us. Room 4127."

Dave's heart started banging around in his chest, and his eyes barely worked. He managed to get them going in the right direction down the hall and around the corner. Of course room 4127 would be the farthest one away, just like the table where he'd met Sissy for their second chance. But soon enough, they stood outside the appointed door, their baby on the other side of it.

The door was closed, and everything felt silent. Reverent. Serene.

She reached for the door handle and went in first, Dave right behind her, his hand on her lower back for comfort.

"Hey, Lola," Sissy said, her voice staying steady and strong.

"Hey, guys," she said from the bed. She wasn't holding the infant girl, and she looked into the plastic bin beside her bed.

Dave couldn't look away from the perfect baby there, swaddled in a white blanket with pink flowers on it. She wore a pale pink hat that contrasted with her dark skin, her eyes pressed closed as she slept.

His heart grew and filled with love. Once, twice, over and over again.

"Can I pick her up?" Sissy asked.

"Of course," Lola said, a tentative smile on her face. "Did you decide on a name?"

Sissy didn't answer as she scooped the little girl into her arms. She faced Dave wearing a smile so big, it filled her whole being. He couldn't help but smile back at her, his eyes filling with tears.

"Evelyn," he managed to say. "It was my grandmother's name."

"That's beautiful," Lola said, watching Sissy and the baby. "I let them know you were coming. All the paperwork is ready."

Gratitude and love moved through him again. "Thank you, Lola." He stepped over to the bed and bent down to hug her. They'd met her several times over the months, and he'd always liked her. But this was a different feeling. She was giving them something they couldn't get on their own. Her sacrifice was not lost on him, and as her tears made his shirt wet, he kept his arms around her.

"Take good care of her," she said, her voice choked.

"We will," he promised. "And it's open, Lola. You can come see her any time you want."

"Any time," Sissy said, her tears streaming down her face. She passed the infant girl to Dave, who marveled at her perfection. She snuggled right into his chest, and he couldn't stop the tear that slid down his cheek.

Sissy too embraced Lola, and he held Evelyn out to her so she could give her biological daughter one last kiss before they left.

Everything happened so fast after that. Dave carried the baby as they went down the hall to the office where the adoption counselor waited for them. Papers were signed, and Sissy carried Evelyn out to the car and lovingly strapped her into the car seat they'd picked out together a couple of weekends ago.

Back in the car, Dave felt completely different. He looked at Sissy, realizing that this was definitely the happiest he'd ever been. "Well."

"We have a baby," she whispered, glancing in the back seat.

"We sure do," he said, leaning over to kiss her.

She cradled his face in both her hands, making him feel cherished and adored. "I love you, Dave."

"I love you too, Sissy."

Read on for a sneak peek at **LAST CHANCE LAKE**, the next book in this series!

Sneak Peek! Last Chance Lake - Chapter One

C ache Bryant sat on the front steps of his cabin, his acoustic guitar across his lap as he watched the sun rise in front of him. The golden rays filled his soul with light and peace, and he loved this time of the morning.

Before dawn, he didn't have to worry about his tasks for today. He didn't worry about the bills he had to pay, or the cows he had to train, or the woman he wanted to impress.

Cache enjoyed the moment while he could, because he had a lot to do today. Scarlett, the owner of Last Chance Ranch, had been hounding him about getting the cow cuddling up and running. She simply had no idea how much it took to make a bovine lay down and be petted. It wasn't natural for cows, though Cache had found that they liked it.

But cows were stubborn, and the training had taken

longer than he'd anticipated. Than anyone had anticipated.

As they were wont to do, his thoughts wandered first to his family's dairy farm in Nevada. They'd lost it a couple of years ago, and Cache had come further west to Last Chance Ranch while his brother and father had gone east and south to Shiloh Ridge in Texas.

Maybe he just needed to go visit them. Get a change of scenery for a few days. He wasn't sure, but the funk he'd fallen into recently seemed to be plaguing him for longer than usual.

He liked his job here at Last Chance Ranch. He did. He loved the people, though he was feeling particularly lonely now that Sawyer was married and Dave had started dating Sissy. Cache felt like so much of his life had passed him by, while he watched the sun rise and milked cows.

But it was his life, and he actually enjoyed it—most of the time.

He sighed as he got to his feet. After taking his guitar inside and propping it in the corner against the coat closet, he grabbed his work gloves from the end table near the couch and headed out.

"Mornin'," Dave said as he moved down his front steps too, and Cache smiled at him.

"Yep, it's morning again," Cache said. They started down the road together, though Dave sometimes drove his truck down to the stables where he worked. Cache had worked jobs all over the ranch, but he'd traded out his time on the south side of the ranch with the bigger animals to administer meds to the horses for the large care vet. And when he wasn't doing that, he worked in the Canine Club or with his dairy cows.

Last Chance Ranch wasn't really set up to be a dairy operation, and his cows' milk had dried up a while ago. They grazed, and lowed at the chickens that got out of their coops, and hopefully, Cache could start getting people into the pasture for the cuddling.

"How are the cows doing?" Dave asked, and it seemed that was all anyone asked Cache.

"Great," he said. "How's the new dog?"

A smile spread across Dave's face. "Awesome. I might get another one."

"They're all over anyway," Cache said, smiling. A couple of cars turned onto the road behind them, and Cache moved to the side. "Goat yoga this morning."

"I don't understand it," Dave said.

"Yeah." Cache said nothing about the cuddling. Until they were ready to launch to program, Scarlett had sworn him to secrecy. She wouldn't even tell Karla, the ranch's marketing director, and surely she'd need time to put together something for the announcement of the program.

Cache wasn't sure. What he knew was limited, only what he could glean from a couple of articles online about a farm in New England. Connecticut, if he remembered right. If there were other farms or ranches picking up on the idea, he hadn't heard of them.

"Band practice Friday?" Dave asked.

"Yeah," Cache said, wishing he had a date on Friday night. He could ask someone, he knew. Plenty of women came to the ranch each day, from volunteers to regular employees like the new veterinarian technician Scarlett had hired a few months ago.

"Got any new songs?" Dave asked, and Cache finally started to feel more like himself.

"Yeah," he said. "And Sawyer's said he'll have one too. Apparently, being awake in the middle of the night with a baby has helped his creativity."

Dave chuckled with Cache. "Yeah, I bet."

"Cute baby they brought home," Cache said.

"Totally," Dave said, keeping his gaze down the road as they passed in front of the homestead.

"I'll see you later," Cache said, detouring to the right while Dave kept going. The administration building was down that way, and Dave had taken to stopping by that building in the morning since he'd started seeing Sissy more often.

Cache hadn't asked him specifically about her, but Dave had been in an increasingly good mood the past month or so, and Sissy had been the only thing in his life that had changed. Cache could put two and two together.

He cleaned out the watering troughs for the llamas and refilled them, enjoying the crisp start to the day. He took a deep breath and got to work measuring the medicines Blade needed that day.

Everything about a living, breathing, working ranch enthralled him, and always had. He loved the circle of life, even when sometimes he lost a horse or a cow or a dog.

After getting all the medicines to all the right equines, he headed back toward the homestead, where his ninety-six dairy cows were housed in a huge field across the stretch from the cabins that bordered the back yard of the homestead.

He couldn't help glancing to the row of cabins there. Gramps lived in the end one, and Cache loved the old man as if he were his own grandfather. Adele and Carson lived in the one in the middle, and Karla Jenkins lived in the third.

Karla Jenkins.

The woman Cache had been trying to impress for a while now. He'd invited her to the Halloween carnival eight months ago so she could see his band. She'd come, and she'd clapped and laughed along with everyone else.

But she hadn't gushed over him the way the girls did to Dave. Cache could sing too, but his first love was the guitar. His second was these insufferable cows, and he jumped over the fence to join them in the pasture.

He whistled at them as if they were dogs, and several turned toward him. "Cookie. Daisy. Come on, girls."

Some of the cows he'd named and could tell them one from another. Only about eight or nine of them, the ones he'd been working with tirelessly to get them to lay down on command.

His cows lumbered toward him, all but two who stayed stubbornly out in the field a ways. He didn't whistle again, as he'd been working for months to get Jenny and Flower to lie down and stay there.

He went to them instead, starting to talk to them the closer he got. "What's going on with you two?" he asked. "Are you sick?"

His other cuddlers came with him, their footsteps heavy in the grass. He avoided a spot of cow manure, asking, "Flower, what are you doing?" He reached the cow and ran his hand down her side. She didn't seem to be bloated.

"What—?" It was then that he saw the sandy blonde hair of a woman curled into the cow's chest.

Karla Jenkins herself tilted her head back and looked up at him. A smile sprang to her face, and she looked like a bright ray of heaven. "Morning."

"Good morning," he said, glad it was a natural reaction and he didn't have to think to do it. Karla Jenkins, out in his cow pasture, cuddling his cows. He had no idea what to make of it.

"What are you doing here?" he asked, staring openly at her. She'd been in his dreams for months, and yet she'd never really indicated that she was interested in him at all.

"Scarlett told me you were training your cows for a cuddling thing," she said. "I thought I'd try it. Is this how it's done?"

Cache wanted to blurt that her cuddling into Flower's

side was one of the sexiest things he'd ever seen. Instead, he just nodded. "They've only had me to practice with," he said.

"I'm happy to volunteer as a test subject," she said.

"You could get kicked."

She smiled at him again. "Oh, I don't think so. This cow is nothing but a sweetheart." She patted Flower's ribcage.

Cache chuckled, some of the awkwardness between him and Karla leaking away. It didn't seem fair, though, that she had to be here, looking so soft and lovely and cuddling with his cow.

Maybe he could just ask her to dinner. He'd never really come out and asked. Maybe he was absolutely terrible at flirting and needed to be more forthright.

"Cache," she said, and he blinked himself back into focusing on her.

"Yeah?"

She stood up and brushed dirt and grass from her clothes. She wore a pair of khaki shorts and a cute T-shirt with lemons on it. "I didn't mean to step on your toes."

"You didn't," he said. "I was just surprised. Scarlett didn't want anyone to know about the cow cuddling."

Karla ran her fingers through her hair, driving Cache toward the brink of madness.

"You wouldn't want to...I don't know. Go to dinner with me. Would you?" Cache swallowed, and he swore Flower sighed as if to say, *Oh, buddy, bad idea.*

Karla blinked, shock traveling across her face in slow waves. "Dinner?"

"Yeah, dinner," Cache said boldly, refusing to look away. No more games. No more dancing around this woman at the meals she cooked for the whole ranch.

The longer she stood there and stared at him, framed by his lounging cows, the stupider Cache felt. Was she going to say anything? He'd even take a no at this point. At least then he'd know.

Still, she said nothing.

Sneak Peek! Last Chance Lake - Chapter Two

Karla Jenkins tried to find the right words and put them in the right order. Cache Bryant had just asked her out. Right out loud. She'd noticed that they'd been flirting on and off for a few months now, and he was brilliant with a guitar in his hands.

And with these cows, as she'd never seen a cow just lie right down and let a human curl into it. But two of his had done exactly that, and she couldn't wait to report back to Scarlett.

"It's fine," Cache said. "Never mind." He turned and started walking away, everything in Karla desperate to call him back. But she just watched as he moved over to a different cow and started talking to it too, in the same human-like way he had Flower.

"Flower," she whispered, stroking her hand down the cow's hide again. "How do I tell him?" She wanted to go out with him, and she was flattered he'd asked. But she had so many things she *didn't* want to talk about. Mistakes from her past. And didn't people talk about their past when they started dating?

Karla hadn't been in the game for a while, but she thought she still knew the rules. And Cache would want to know about her, and she'd have to tell him things if she wanted to keep him in her life.

The two sides of herself went to war, and she honestly had no idea which one would win. The man—the ridiculously handsome cowboy—in question glanced over to her, and Karla still stood there, unsure about what to do.

She wasn't sure if her heart could take another battering. "Maybe he'll be gentle with your heart," she whispered to herself. Yeah, and maybe he could train these cows to fly. She didn't think so, but she needed to explain.

She stepped around the legs of the cow and headed toward him. "Cache," she said just as he snuggled into the side of a cow.

"Come join me," he said. "I want them to be able to tolerate two people."

"Cache," she repeated, and he gestured for her to come over.

She did, stepping between the hooves and sitting on the ground next to Cache. Their eyes met, and he was so, so handsome. Her breath caught in her throat, and she found herself diving all the way into his blue, blue eyes.

"Good girl, Cookie," he said, patting the cow.

"Do you have names for all of them?" she asked.

"Just a few," he said. "The several I've been working with on the cuddling."

"How do you pick them?"

"Well, all the cows are girls," he said. "So I just call them whatever. Daisy or Flower. Bluebell. Floral varieties are popular, obviously." He put that delightful smile on his face, and Karla's heart started bobbing somewhere in the back of her throat.

They sat in silence for a minute, and Karla decided maybe she could be honest with him. "Cache, I want to go out with you."

He turned his head and looked at her. "Are you sure?"

"Of course I'm sure. I just...." She gazed at the horizon. "This might sound stupid, but I don't want to be the talk of the ranch if we start seeing each other."

"Is that what would happen?" Cache asked, his phone buzzing.

"Possibly, and I—I'm a pretty private person."

"It's okay," Cache said, getting to his feet. "I have to get over to Piggy Paradise. I'll see you later, okay?" He didn't wait for Karla to say anything before he dashed off.

She stayed against the cow's side and gazed up into the cloudless California sky. She wanted to pray for help, but she didn't quite know how. She'd tried that before anyway, and nothing much had come from it.

She'd still lost her job. Her husband. Her baby.

The pain that always came when she allowed this

particular box to open sliced through her. She'd gotten a new job. A better job. She loved Last Chance Ranch, and it had come with the cabin that had allowed her to truly get a new start on her life.

She didn't want the husband anymore, and that really was a problem. Jackson had been terrible for her from the beginning, and she'd been a fool to think a baby could fix their broken marriage.

In the end, she'd lost both, and most of her life felt like a waste. She'd managed to put together a few pieces, but it had come at a high price. A vow that she didn't need a man in her life, something she'd kept since the divorce had been finalized five years ago.

Could she break that vow now? For a cheerful cowboy with the best eyes she'd ever seen?

She sighed as she got up too. "Thanks for the cuddle, Cookie."

LATER THAT DAY, Karla sat at her desk in her office, which was really the second bedroom in the cabin on the edge of the homestead's backyard. She hadn't made lunch for the ranch workers that day. She'd hardly gotten any work done either.

All she'd been able to do was sit at the desk and stare as she thought about Cache Bryant and his dinner invitation.

He'd taken it off the table and never really put it back on before running off to do his job. She had his phone number. She could call him. But she had no idea what to say.

"Focus," she muttered to herself, and she looked down at her computer. She was supposed to be putting up next month's goat yoga schedule, and she couldn't seem to get it done.

After that, she needed to confirm with Forever Friends about the Fourth of July picnic and adoption event, taking place in a couple of months. That event should be highly publicized around the ranch and through the Forever Friends organization, and Karla had a meeting the following day that would take her down to the offices in LA.

Anxiety hit her at having to return to the city. All those memories. All those people. But she pushed aside the panic and picked up her phone to text Vicky, the only friend she had left from her previous life.

Still on for lunch tomorrow?

Yes! Vic's text came back almost immediately. Karla smiled at her device as they confirmed their location and time. Then Karla would drive back to the ranch, back to this small cabin, back to this simpler, easier life.

Karla loved this life, but she'd started to feel like it was hollow. She was a shell, with nothing of substance inside.

And her thoughts went back to Cache again. Wondering if he could provide some sort of fulfillment for her, Karla once again stalled in her work. Could she really find out? She'd heard all of the love stories here on the ranch—and if he didn't think they'd be the source of all gossip if they even so much as glanced at each other with a playful glint in their eyes, he was sorely mistaken—and she didn't want to feel like she couldn't be here if she and Cache started something and broke up.

She didn't need to repeat what had happened in the city.

Keep it a secret.

Words that Scarlett had said to her that morning, regarding the cow cuddling Cache had been doing in the pasture right across the lane from her cabin. Apparently, he'd been working with his cows for a long time, and she hadn't known.

But now, her brain was suggesting she keep her relationship with Cache a secret. She scoffed out loud. There was *no* relationship with Cache.

"Yet," she muttered under her breath. And maybe if she could get him to ask her to dinner again, she could suggest they go, sure. But that no one else could know.

Satisfied with that solution, Karla was finally able to get some work done.

"GIRL, YOU HAVE LOST WEIGHT," Vic said when Karla walked into the restaurant where they'd agreed to meet for lunch.

She scoffed. "I have not." She hugged her friend. "If anything, I've gained ten pounds feeding everyone on the ranch."

"You were always a genius with feeding large groups." Vic nodded to the hostess, and she grabbed two menus and took them back to a table. "I miss that about you around the office."

Karla put a smile on her face and nodded. "I don't miss much about the city," she said. "I can handle coming for a meeting, but I don't want to live or work here." And not only because she might run into Jackson.

"How'd the meeting go?" Vic asked, getting situated on the bench across from Karla. "You're working with that animal sanctuary, right?"

"Right," Karla said. "It went great. I love the people there. They have a real passion for saving abandoned or injured animals."

Vic smiled and nodded, and Karla needed to change the subject. She loved her friend, but Vic didn't understand how Karla could leave the city and be happy. Sometimes Karla couldn't believe it either.

"So there's a new band I'm into," Karla said, and Vic's face lit up. She enjoyed lunch with her friend, but she didn't ask any questions about Karla's life. Didn't ask if she was seeing anyone new, or had made any friends, or if she liked the cabin she'd been living in for almost a year.

As she hugged her BFF good-bye, Karla couldn't help but think that the relationship had turned...hollow. Just like everything else in her life.

She kept the radio off as she drove back to Last Chance Ranch, hoping some inspiration would strike her. Or maybe lightning. At this point, Karla would take almost anything.

As she drove up the dirt road to the ranch, she noticed someone had put a pair of bunny ears on the robot that stood sentinel at the entrance. She smiled at them, a little ray of hope in her otherwise dreary existence.

She wasn't sure why they were there, as Easter had come and gone last month. But it didn't matter. Karla drove down the road to the back of her cabin, parked, and got out, the bunny ears reminding her that even the simplest of things mattered.

She mattered.

To who, she wasn't sure, but she could start with Scarlett and Hudson. They depended on her to get promotional activities ready for the ranch. Maintain the website. Feed the people on the ranch.

They needed her.

Even if God had abandoned her. Even if Jackson had left in the middle of the night. Even if she'd walked into her job one morning and walked out an hour later, all her stuff in a pathetic, brown box.

Her phone chimed, and she pulled it out of her purse to check it.

Hey, Karla, Cache had texted. *Do you have a sec? I need to talk to you about something.*

A smile pulled at the corners of her mouth.

Cache needed her, too.

Can Cache capture Karla's heart through...cow cuddling?
Read LAST CHANCE LAKE today to find out!

Scan the QR code for a direct link to the paperback.

Last Chance Ranch Romance series

Journey to Last Chance Ranch and meet curvy, mature women looking for love later in life. Experience sisterhood, goat yoga, and a fake marriage against a stunning, inspirational ranch background—and some sexy cowboys too— from USA Today bestseller and Top 10 Kindle All-Star author Liz Isaacson!

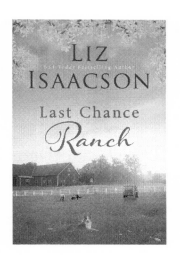

Last Chance Ranch (Book 1): A cowgirl down on her luck hires a man who's good with horses and under the hood of a car. Can Hudson fine tune Scarlett's heart as they work together? Or will things back-fire and make everything worse at Last Chance Ranch?

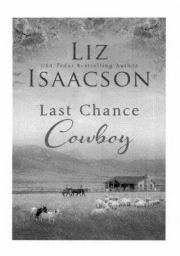

Last Chance Cowboy (Book 2): A billionaire cowboy without a home meets a woman who secretly makes food videos to pay her debts...Can Carson and Adele do more than fight in the kitchens at Last Chance Ranch?

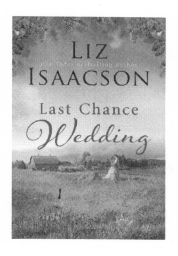

Last Chance Wedding (Book 3): A female carpenter needs a husband just for a few days... Can Jeri and Sawyer navigate the minefield of a pretend marriage before their feelings become real?

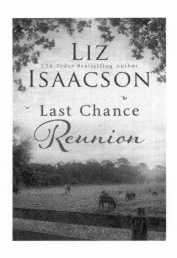

Last Chance Reunion (Book 4): An Army cowboy, the woman he dated years ago, and their last chance at Last Chance Ranch... Can Dave and Sissy put aside hurt feelings and make their second chance romance work?

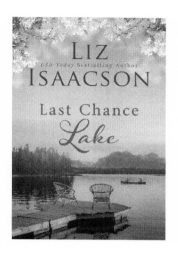

Last Chance Lake (Book 5): A former dairy farmer and the marketing director on the ranch have to work together to make the cow cuddling program a success. But can Karla let Cache into her life? Or will she keep all her secrets from him - and keep *him* a secret too?

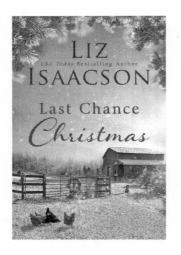

Last Chance Christmas (Book 6): She's tired of having her heart broken by cowboys. He waited too long to ask her out. Can Lance fix things quickly, or will Amber leave Last Chance Ranch before he can tell her how he feels?

About Liz

Liz Isaacson writes inspirational romance, usually set in Texas, or Montana, or anywhere else horses and cowboys exist. She lives in Utah, where she walks her dogs daily, watches a lot of Netflix, and eats a lot of peanut butter M&Ms while writing. Find her on her website at feelgood-fictionbooks.com.

Made in the USA
Las Vegas, NV
18 November 2022

59750252R00146